SILENCE

Rodney Hall is one of Australia's finest writers. He has won the Miles Franklin twice, for *Just Relations* and *The Grisly Wife,* and many of his novels and poems have been published internationally. His acclaimed memoir *popeye never told you* was published in 2010. He lives in Melbourne.

Other books by the author include

The Ship on the Coin
A Place among People
Just Relations
Kisses of the Enemy
Captivity Captive
The Second Bridegroom
The Grisly Wife
The Island in the Mind
The Day We Had Hitler Home
The Last Love Story
Love Without Hope
popeye never told you

SILENCE

[fictions]

RODNEY HALL

Published in Australia in 2011 by Pier 9,
an imprint of Murdoch Books Pty Limited

Murdoch Books Australia
Pier 8/9
23 Hickson Road
Millers Point NSW 2000
Phone: +61 (0) 2 8220 2000
Fax: +61 (0) 2 8220 2558
www.murdochbooks.com.au
info@murdochbooks.com.au

Murdoch Books UK Limited
Erico House, 6th Floor
93–99 Upper Richmond Road
Putney, London SW15 2TG
Phone: +44 (0) 20 8785 5995
Fax: +44 (0) 20 8785 5985
www.murdochbooks.co.uk
info@murdochbooks.co.uk

Publisher: Melanie Ostell
Editor: Ali Lavau
Designer: Tania Gomes
Production: Joan Beal

National Library of Australia
Cataloguing-in-Publication entry:

Hall, Rodney, 1935–
Silence / Rodney Hall.
978-1-74266-591-7 (pbk.)
A823.3

Printed in Australia by Griffin Press, an Accredited ISO AS/NZS 14001:2004
Environmental Management System printer.

FSC
www.fsc.org
MIX
Paper from
responsible sources
FSC® C009448

For Ian Dixon, friend and filmmaker

I felt like answering him in the words of the dying Amr: 'I feel as if heaven lay close upon the earth and I between them both, breathing through the eye of a needle.'

Lawrence Durrell, *Justine*

Contents

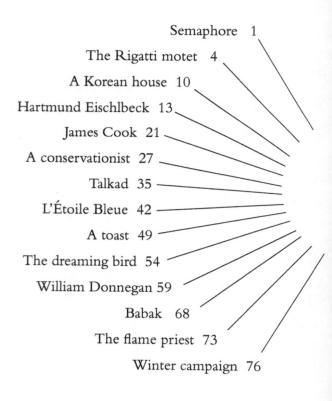

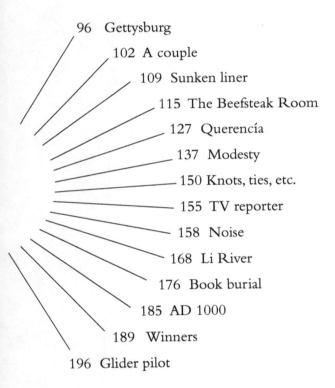

Semaphore

A man jumped up on the horizon. Quite suddenly he jumped up where nobody had been before. A soldier with nothing on his head to protect it. In the afternoon. Behind him a massive slagheap of cloud gathered. And above the cloud three parachutes seemed fixed in the sky. The big guns had already fallen silent and every last aircraft had long since flown away. It was on a ridge above some straight shadows that were the enemy trenches. And up he jumped.

And there was one who asked: Do we shoot him, Sergeant Potts?

But Sergeant Potts just spat. Spat on the ground.

Because this was something no one could account for, a soldier making a target of himself in full view of the platoon of hidden men in helmets, each one of us with his finger on the trigger and a question in his eyes. Each one homesick from too much bitterness and loss. And too much fear felt too soon. Boy soldiers, rookies, with no idea what to do next.

Someone whispered: It must be a trick.

Or else a lunatic, another whispered back and opened the wound of a grin in his face.

Another asked: What are they going to chuck at us next?

But Sergeant Potts poked around under the rim of his helmet and scratched his skull.

All because a man jumped up where nobody had been before. Quite suddenly dark and small in the afternoon, with nothing to protect his head and only the cloud beyond. And three parachutists fixed in the sky above while we hid, watching him, a platoon of boys in baggy uniforms. Boys with no idea what to do. And this man, who was our enemy, lifted wooden arms. Slow as a broken windmill he started signalling. One letter at a time he spelt out a message in semaphore: ICH HABE HUNGER.

The Rigatti motet

Friar Fidelis stood rigid, not able to move, suffocated by exhausted air. He and the rest of the choir had been packed into a globe of darkness, itself cupped in obscurity, suspended far above the altar, right up inside the dome of Brunelleschi's vast dim cathedral. They waited in this huge pod, this theatrical contraption—the tenors grouped around him, the basses immediately beneath his feet and the boys above his head—in a dangling machine already filled with intolerable heat. And the waiting, which began calmly enough as a meditation on God's divine presence, despite an unthinkable drop beneath them, had soon become a nightmare. The contraption a form of torture. No one should be asked to endure such danger and discomfort. They were not heretics, after all. The planned spectacle, in honour of the cardinal's enthronement, more appropriate to opera. The theatre architect responsible, also rumoured to be an associate of the illustrious Signor Galileo, deserved to be strung up by his heels!

His own rancour took Friar Fidelis by surprise and alarmed him. He had lapsed into sin.

The last whispers fell silent. So might he, too, have been whispering? Without realising it? Perhaps others knew of his resentment. He must suppress all trace of anger. By which, of course, he meant all trace of fear. His fellow choristers from the monastery of Santa Maria Novella, dressed like himself in thick white habits, could be smelt hanging on to their nerve and only just controlling the contagious waves of hysteria given out by the boys among them. The staleness of used breath gagged him, nose and mouth. He called on his training in submission. Drenched with sweat and unable to tell whether his eyes were shut or open, he let his damp hands find one another in prayer.

Surrendering in that plug of utter blackness, he encouraged his mind to glide over the contours of a musical phrase, the first notes of what must soon be sung. But did he still have a voice? Did any of them have voices? Had so much effort of rehearsal—not to mention the effort of constructing this suspended chamber they were in—been wasted? The very idea of shutting a blind and voiceless choir in a contraption that might never open out to the congregation's astonishment showed itself as folly and vanity.

Little could be heard of the service below apart from wordless echoes punctuated by the tiny metallic intervals of the cruet and the hand bell. A suspicion dawned on him: the great occasion was destined to end in failure and humiliation, the cardinal unenthroned, the city disgraced in the eyes of the Pope. Yes, the Holy Father himself was down there. Yes, with the perilous weight of a theatrical device dangling high above his venerable head (and what would be in that head if not all-encompassing compassion for the sufferers?). Friar Fidelis gasped for air. He was at the point of fainting when the shell cracked open.

Sudden vertical slashes of light began to gape around him.

Alarmingly fast, the ribs of the machine creaked ajar to pivot on the principle of an upside-down umbrella, clefts disclosed random slices of the scenes painted on the walls: elephantine sinners being tortured in hell, shitting flames and biting hunks of silence from the surrounding fire, one damned soul tearing his own flesh open like an unbuttoned shirt to let a pearly ball of intestines tumble out. As Friar Fidelis descended, his personal puff of wooden cloud unfolding from the huge collective cloud that had suffocated him, demons with shaggy thighs and outspread wings drifted up, away, and out of sight. So, the choristers sank in unison, perilously perpendicular like wobbly candles in a candelabrum. Intent on keeping his balance, Friar Fidelis, nonetheless, relived the flickering glory of an airborne child in its father's arms.

Ambrosial incense sucked at his lungs in a painful spasm. The monumental creaking of the structure as it shuddered earthward filled him with reborn panic. He knew how far they would fall if they fell. He had several times climbed the hundreds of stairs to visit the gallery in this dome. Not to mention the dizzying illusion of inlaid patterns set into the floor so it would seem to plunge a further three storeys deeper. Right now he dared not look down. Gripping a handle provided by the architect, he inhaled deeply while fixing his mind on prayer. Gratefully, he knew how. He had the words and the vocation. Such was his life and he wished for no other.

The time had come. The spokes of the machine extended to a colossal dandelion head and, quivering, stopped.

The choir, after their collective swooping descent, jolted to a standstill among muted rays of daylight from the high windows. Candle flames trembled palely around them as the cantor sang the offertory verse. Friar Fidelis felt his soul soar across that sublime space ... now singing, just as the others sang, a harmony so perfect, so rich with interwoven elaborations, tears filled his eyes. In that mighty cry of jubilation it was as if he heard his name spoken. They were angels, indeed (and must seem so from down in the nave), suspended, each in his own alcove of heaven. Maestro Rigatti's motet evolved as pure mathematics given voice, an anatomy of the mind, the joyful embodiment of faith. Anno 1638.

So, harmonies emerged from harmony and individual voices were lost in the whole. Friar Fidelis could not tell whether he was singing or not. His entire being vibrated as he surrendered to the greater surrender of the expansive *Amen* now filling that cavernous cathedral and giving life, with its incremental climax, to every atom of stone and glass, till nothing could be heard but the prismatic elements of silence.

A Korean house

The doors are open. Folded quilts have been stacked on cupboards and the wrapping cloths—modest works of art—put away in drawers. Cushions in their loose covers are stored on brassbound chests. Paper-screened shutters, pinned back, show polished floors and the scrupulous order of the house. Fallen leaves slide down the roof's raked gutters: blood-red maple leaves on the tiles, these and the gingko's little golden fans have begun heaping up and clogging the downpipes. The last servant to leave, a cloth mask covering her nose and mouth, a swishing brush in her hand, erases her own footprints as she retreats, leaving the gravel yard perfect, untrodden, even while embers die in the grates and a final wisp of smoke escapes the chimneys, the warmed *ondol* floors left to grow cold. This is how a Korean nobleman's house should look, canopied in autumnal glory and reflected in still ponds. She has gone. She has left the birdwinged roofs behind. The whole structure hovers. Such perfect openness, such quiet, she believes, will shock the Japanese invader into recognizing his intrusion as a crime.

Hartmund Eischlbeck

The tragedy of it is Hartmund Eischlbeck has inherited his famous grandfather's nose, poor unfortunate, as well as his voice, but not his grandfather's intelligence, no, no—nor his colossal bottlenosed ambition—neither of them worth a cracker anyway to Hartmund, who never discovered a vocation of his own. Is now thirty-six and faced with life's downward slope. Despite which, he builds a tower singlehanded. Yes, huge windowless tower it gives you the creeps to think of. Dresses the stone blocks, mixes mortar, climbs the scaffold and sets in place seventy courses of diminishing circumference, by Jesus. Half a lifetime's work for any normal fanatic.

Culmination being these last few days of building, the *finale banale*, as he himself jokes being rather gifted in this department and is sufficiently amused. Must be admitted, though, Hartmund Eischlbeck, for the most part faultlessly grim, is working under extreme difficulty. Well, because the weather man sends rain, an overflow beyond the regional average, courtesy of ABC Television. Rampant isobars. Sensational unseasonal not to say impertinent rain. Watersmelling and ironcorroding. Each drop of it a plumbline from cloudheight to landform. And all a conspiracy to swirl together for the purpose of trapping our hero in a colossal and colossally noisy vortex. Which, by the way, is colossally wet too.

Local witnesses, hurrying for shelter, fugitives every one, report Eischlbeck, twenty metres above their respectable heads, atop his tower with lightning flashes in his hair.

He, shiny steel face in-turned on the task at hand, notices no one. Certainly not those bloody nonentities. Nor the log trucks, inaudible gears grinding, chipmill-bound, headlights aglow in broad daydark. Nor a car smash acted out in silence at the crossroads way beneath. Preoccupied by the task in hand. Alone. O mother! Hard-mooned, heart-moaned. Eis. Locked out by memories. Reminded of a drowned forest and young life he never had. Of careless youthful rapture missed. And missed again as more or less an adult. Of caution not thrown to the winds. The common touch eluding him. Not just the large thing of love but the lesser thing of neighbourliness too. The life of others. So, he labours on his tower. Dense spiralled curtains of rain bounce and glitter around him as he works in deafened isolation: Aurora Australis in black and white—as illustrated in his old between-the-wars encyclopaedia.

Somewhere in *Memories, Dreams, Reflections* Carl G. Jung extols the satisfaction of building a tower. Well, Hartmund Eischlbeck suspects the towerbuilder Jung was a man demanding satisfactions of a high order. His own tower, even so, is dedicated to a less selfish function than the psychologist's sunlit study. His is a casket, a reliquary, a lightless and permanently sealed monument. An embodiment. And therefore—one in the eye for CG!—a symbol! Around the foot of the scaffolding, his worksite dump of masonry in broken bits, mallets, brackets and off-cut planks left over from the task and cement bags stacked against the wall.

Hartmund Eischlbeck has built a tower. And in that tower it is going to seal his patrimony of a family tradition, that's what. Mementos and such. Gifts left him in his grandfather's will, the whole codonomy of it all.

Terrible accumulations of stuff he has no use for. The slights and wounds he has suffered too. All to be shut away forever in this phallic tomb. He's a prudent member and no mistake. Therefore an end to grandfather, father and self. Instance, that grandfather, the archetypal shaper of autobamboozling theories—whiskers and long white locks more appropriate among Michelangelo clouds than the streets of Bangywallop—the celebrated missionary immortalized as a mountain range on the maps. But God knows where! The father another such with such another bottlenose and about as much sympathy for the fraternity of mudpuddlers and factoryfodder as for the authors of the Book of Ballymote. Poor Hartmund (as should be sufficiently clear). Sole heir to a family treasure of artefacts, notes and recordings that the National Museum urges him to donate to them. Bag and baggage: boomerangs, headgear, woven baskets still stink-struck from the fish, cowrie necklaces, sacred messages in the old man's mumbo-jumbo (the decoding of which is believed to be punishable with death by bone-pointing), ritual shields, kadaitcha boots and so forth. And enough fieldnotes in longhand to fill the catacombs of Rome. Plus an index of exhibits crossreferenced with the 'wordbook' his great-grandfather garnered from native Australians before helping stamp out the very language he had spent his life collecting. Ah, to live a shadow of life. Plato's dream. Ghosts. Is extinction ever final? Well, doing his bit, Hartmund seals away the remains of a culture eradicated by blessings. An end to the curse bequeathed him as a boy. Sea-sounds in a hundred empty shells. All his to keep, by order of a last will and testament. Treasures caked with red soil and dusted with dust. These for starters. Heaps more, too. Container loads of lethal junk.

Himself balanced precariously at the basalt rim, he might conveniently topple to his death at any moment. O, where is thy sting? Where the mystery? Up on that doorless windowless tower whose only opening is the hole at the top that he labours right now to close, he doesn't hear the police car arrive at the scene of the crash down there, let alone himself discussed by those in uniform. Defying the storm like one possessed, Hartmund Eischlbeck fits block after block in place. The end in reach. The past securely shut away and sealed. Grandson of the grandfather—nose of the nose: a nose familiar to the collective memory of a nomad nation far inland as the mark of a thief—who, in his final triumph over C.G. Jung, pulls back the tarpaulin for one last look. Down inside his tower he can barely make out the timber storage shelves and dark chambers. All packed full.

Twilight of goodbye under sagging cloud. Storehouse of his misfortune. A structure, proof against prying or theft.

The beehived courses, stone on stone, narrow as a chimney, hug his knees as he works. Hair, overalls and shirt plastered to his skull and bones. Plagued by memories: sea-sickness once, and the falling dream, being stranded on stage at school with his lines forgotten and the fourth-form audience tittering, his failed romances at the boatshed formal, crashing a glider, his travels and the hardships of smalltalk in tourist coaches at ancient Borsippa, himself on the eroded knoll where Nabu once stood and the biblical tower E-ur-iminan-ki so famously doomed because the labourers slaved amid too great a cataract of smalltalk in jumbled languages to put together a decent lawless mutiny.

No, no, Hartmund Eischlbeck does not neglect the family religion.

So, with his cold chisel he chips the last stone for a perfect fit. Even, at the final stroke, the finishing touch, blinded by rain. Gashes his hand. The chisel falls inside a long way down. Clink. A gift for some archaeologist a thousand years hence. Balanced on the coping he slides the slab in place. Perfect. Pauses. He stands tall against a glassbead sky. Rainwater rills and froths, cascading down the courses of stone.

Hartmund has thought it out. The legacy will stand, untouched, untouchable, on private land, safe in family hands, willed to an unsuspecting nephew in Koblenz—on condition the contents remain shut away in perpetuity. Scion of the house of Eischlbeck, Hartmund has the strength and the ready cash. The crown stone weighing not much less than himself now snugly seated. Trowel scraping the excess from the last of the mortar. He faces about and blesses gravely thrice the tower, the surrounding country and the awaking mountains (all but erased from the skyline) as rain and more rain rains and thunder crashes stupendously. He does not hear the Mental Institute ambulance arrive, nor paramedics slamming doors. Nor sodden boots plod in through his gate.

James Cook

The wind off the land has droppd alltogether, *Resolution*'s rigging steady as compass-bearings ruled upon the sky. The stillness is intense, tho, for myself, memories of yesterday's shots spoil all peace of mind. We can guess who fired them—but at whom? Why did they stop? Why has Mr Cook not yet returnd? In our hearts we suspect he has met his death. This is our tremendous reason for idleness, unable to decide what might be done. Moreover, any false action could be construed by the natives as incivility if, in fact, he is yet alive. Having taken a powder-horn from my pouch to be ready, prudently I slip it back out of sight of the crew.

Captn Clerke objects that Mr Cook could surely have come to no harm, it being barely two weeks since he was ceremoniously welcomd here. Indeed, the islanders robed him then in a cape of feathers plucked from rare parrots—little orange and yellow chaps—to receive him off our ship like a god. Notwithstanding which, something is unquestionably gone wrong, something which we fear to speak of. Neither I, nor any man aboard, can doubt it & a sullen silence locks down, the cosmos fixd around us on this glassy lagoon.

No sign of natives, tho yesterday we purchased from them two hogs and ten chicken, besides divers fruits and edible berrys. Doubtless they understand some thing we English, being outlandish visitors, cannot guess. Our men, allthough instructed to remain calm, must feel, as do I myself, a tremor through the soles of their feet and throughout their very bones, skeleton & skull: the after-shocks from Saturday's volcano when lava gushed in molten cliffs to explode upon contact with the sea, water being tossd high above the roaring rocks, banks of steam thrown up to billow back across the island with the choking stench of sulphur. Myself sick all day the next two days. Captn Clerke and I put our heads together in the account of it for the ship's log and spent much diligence on an accurate description in the cause of science.

Small bright birds dart across the warm, placid water, screeching as they go, and disappear into the jungle leaving behind them the empty arch of sky. The customary chanting voices from villages among the trees have ceased. Our men stand ready on deck, their musquets being an article seldom far from reach.

We are accustomd to the sun sinking of a sudden toward the horizon in these latitudes, today being no different. Tho in the last moments of setting light the company's attention is diverted by seeing a canoe set out from the shore. Two islanders paddle our way. This much seems clear: their purpose is solemn. Paddles dip in sinister clear water. The swift progres of that tiny craft, across an underwater gulph, furnishes a sight inscribed in the mind like etching on a crystal dish. Drawing near, the paddlers may be seen as wellmade & strong, tho not presenting themselves groomed the way we are accustomed to see them—I have spoke of this elsewhere—these having matted locks and bowed heads. They shine with sweat as the canoe manoeuvres, broadside on, to bring them beneath *Resolution*'s rail where they share the task of holding up a parcel bound in cloath. Captn Clerke reaches down for it, appearing to find it more awkward than expected so the bosun must needs steady his elbow.

A native boy on the shore emerges from concealment, dresst in a red kind of jacket seeming gay and warlike. I am reminded of the dancing women wearing this very colour who once put pebbles on their tongues while their fingers inticed us with lascivious gestures. He throws a rock in our direction. Immediatly following the tiny splash comes the close bang of a musquet inconsiderately fir'd by one of our company. The boy, on the instant, vanishes back among the leaves from whence he came. Thus does our situation alter. The paddlers look up in alarm, tho why at me in particular? We are a far cry from the goodhumourd trade we thought so well established, with bargaining and laughter and an exchange of goods. The parcel is laid on deck.

The canoe slips off from our side to head back across the lagoon: every inscription of the disturbd water in its wake rememberd. As duty demands, I give orders that the men stay calm, even knowing (as who does not?) they have been led where they had no mind to go in the first place. They glower, but none repeats the blunderer's gunshot.

The world attends. Captn Clerke peels the flap of cloath wrapping, so as it should seem to be sticky with blood, to disclose a haunch of meat. The meat, having white skin and coarse black hairs, is a human thigh rarely exposd to the sun, the thickness being carved to remove the bone before delivry. Such, then, is their heathen ritual, to the best of my understanding—this would seem to be due portion of our commander for eating, accordingly explaind elsewhere by missionaries—as with a will of its own, the thigh, sliced lengthwise, gapes open and unfolds like the calyx of a grossly fleshy flower.

A conservationist

Silence is the rock where I shall stand.
The silence between this and the next breath,
that might be—is not yet—death;
the silence between lover and lover
that neither flesh nor mind bridge over;
the silence between word and word,
in which the truth waits to be heard ...

Deafness crept up on the poet out of the shadows of
her garden and the shadows of the engulfing bush
and even the shadows of the city too, when she went
there. Trees tossed by the gale, lightning-lit thunder

clouds and swirling creeks, traffic on rutted gravel and potholes, dark gutters, office blocks, wharves, towers and pointed roofs, all mounted about her and collapsed into black prisms of silence, so she must live in a wilderness within the wider wilderness, isolated from friends and alone among enemies. She must make do with her own company and feminine self-sufficiency, practical in the face of declining faculties, for besides the deafness she was seriously shortsighted too, through days on the cusp of decay when the sun set in an explosion of rosy light and the heavy marble moon hung poised above her head. She sought comfort in what remained to her, the scent of earth, the feel of damp loam. Touched by bridal veils of mist and the frog-spawn dew, she walked around her property 'Edge', singing within herself by way of prayer, though whether any sound escaped her throat she had no means of knowing. Dusk brought the sweetness of busy insects and the whisk of an owl's wing—for she glimpsed its old demanding face among the leaves—the high night of her land wheeling and filled with a harmony of symbols. Even in her sleep she was known to wander through the threat of the unheard till the sun rose, she tasted a new morning and, with a glint of superiority in her eye, placed hands on things for the blessing of texture, on tree bark and grass, on fur and stone. The rocks and vegetation were her neighbours. Those others, relatives and strangers alike, shuttled around in the same belljar as the many who thought her mad and dangerous. Shunned by some and admired by others for having defied a rapacious government and stood up to multinationals in the fight to save the Great Barrier Reef from drilling, she shopped for weekly supplies at the local store where she was known with a neutral kind of familiarity.

Her contempt for her enemies took the form of fierce pity that they had no choice but to live as prisoners of their own greed. Yet her reputation worried at her heels because, the world's vice being persistence, she was not left in peace. A clutch of small-scale goldmines staked their claim right outside her gate. She challenged their permits, she harrassed them in court and in the press. If any of the businessmen involved thought they were dealing with a dotty old lady who could be shut up or bought off they soon learnt otherwise. She would not be browbeaten but she paid the price. That rare and precious private time when, under her eyelids, she caught sickles of the mystery, when the unheard whispers of antecedents, whose suffering through a thousand years of courageous resilience gave her strength, dwindled. She spent what time she could marvelling at the day, luxurious spaces of light and cloud, open, all breathless, immense and clearer than glass, and her feet became distant messengers, attentive to the land, wallaby tracks guiding her in solitude to her own door, where she must shake the radiance from her hair before she could recognise herself in the characteristic oddities shown her by the mirror. I am old, she told it, old and lonely. However, she added, I have been loved and I do love.

She accepted the desk's invitation to sit at it while enormous shadows comforted her with words for writing down and words to be contemplated as creatures, each one with unique habits and habitat: burrowing words and hopping words, words that flew and words that clung to walls weathering storms. Sometimes she need only switch on the lamp to know what needed saying. Words greater than governments. And then followed the days of quiet committed work, all space filled with the ballooning universe, trees signalling and a serpent of light from along the creek curling at her feet, warm and attentive as a dog. And down in the waterhole platypuses paddled sleekly among bent reflections. Flocks of parrots settled in the eucalyptus leaves, swaying voluptuously, brilliant as tropical flowers, only to take flight with an unheard protest of voiceless open beaks when she stood up.

She could not be persuaded, nor could she be corrupted. And if ever she needed reassurance, the deafness itself taught her the bitter injustice of the way things are: she cared nothing for money or fame. She would simply have her say, when meetings were held in the shabby dimness of a local hall, raising her arm to be counted and then sipping afternoon tea among the faithful. Amused by the moth-eaten grandeur of plush stage curtains and timber walls leaking light, she could watch the whole interior open around her as a continent of ramshackle distances, a fantastic Promised Land, malleable, the light buttery enough to be shaped by hand. She signed her name and this was good enough.

She took for granted that there were probably rural bumblings and committee heroics going on, relieved not to know the details. The fact of the matter was that decision remained individual, she disliked crusades and reform movements and pressure groups dedicated to preventing any change at all. Still, respecting the dependability of steps and stages—as the undeaf could hardly be expected to appreciate while distracted from clear thinking by minds filled with a jumble of noise— she played her part and spoke of endangered species to visiting forest rangers, though at all times ready to rise to her feet without preamble, eloquent as a fighting prophet, to let fly till the meeting around her broke out in a frantic activity of mute clapping. A little shamefaced at such times, because she recognised certainty as thinner than paper and as fragile, she consulted a jury of dignified ancestors who'd had the courage to do what needed to be done in times gone by, to say what had needed to be said, however uncomfortable. But the trouble was that all of them, with their direct gaze and a flash of villainy in their seriousness, were well and thoroughly buried in the graveyard under fallen crosses and noseless angels.

Often at night the funny side of her affliction would strike her, recollecting, for instance, a very different afternoon tea, this one with the president of India at his palace in New Delhi, when she took up what she thought he had said and complimented his nation on its agricultural traditions and the maintenance of fertility over millennia of cultivation—'soil so cared for looks good enough to eat!'—which clearly stopped him in his tracks. She later learnt that he had asked her a question about poetry. But her memory of twinkling baffled unrufflable goodwill in his eyes was enough for her to smile now, as she fell asleep, at ease with the absurd blunders of guesswork. Until, next morning, she stepped fresh from the shower. The sight of her own living room shocked her. Unbelievably—and all around—evidence leapt to the eye. As if time escaped the tyranny of sequence chairs were in the wrong place, a vase where she never put it, books and papers rearranged. Everything neat and nothing missing. Her house had been broken into: a warning eloquent enough, even without the fax machine delivering a message. *So you're up. Good morning. You can't hear us. And nobody can hear you … that is to say, apart from us.*

She did swing round, then, this fearless woman. To. To see. To see who might be lurking … and, in doing so, took her first giddy step into the corrupted Terra Incognita of her antagonists.

Talkad

Jottings, impressions and (I suppose) speculations. Here goes:
5 May. Hot. This place was quite a project with stone-
lined streets etc embedded in the jungle. The temple.
Built two days' pilgrimage from Mysore. Stifling heat.
In Karnatakan forest. Treetops bunched globes of leaves
more solid than solid black cloud blanketing the earth.
Pilgrims filing beneath along gloomy paths. Ecstasy of
arrival no doubt. For the first thousand years anyway.
Light that crept in across the floor around squat columns.
Low ceiling very characteristic. Old old and heavy. Once
were craftsmen peeling lengths of sandalwood. Aromatic.
Images in dark corners. Panoply and stuff accumulated

from countless annual processions. All left standing propped at odd angles. Glowering masks included, with shadowy brows and peacock plumes. Human skulls. Garlands of skulls strung across the third eye. Ropes of dessicated marigolds. Great heads sprouting matted locks worn-out like old hemp. Obscure whispers of neglect. Too deep for birdsong. No verses on ritual days. Barefoot worshippers padding across the flagstones. Flagstones waxed with human oil lustre round the shrine to Shiva. Massive lingam. Carved cleft. The god's own phallus to be anointed with liquid ghee. Their devotions. Shiva as World-destroyer, from whom nothing hidden. Stale, moist, opaque. Ritual: the priest handing a tiny silver ladle of water to each arrival. Precious liquid to be cast over their heads. The god witnessing in person. Not like Christianity. No notion of symbols as objects of worship. Hindu gods inhabit their statues. Birth and decorum, sex and death.

Talkad the place is called.

Flourished give-or-take a thousand years while change of climate got to work killing the forest. The dark cloud of leaves soon gone. Dead trees toppled. Foot up. Salt on the surface and ground plants shrivelled. Wind stirred parched soil to rise up as dust storms. Seen for miles around. Until just one last copse of trees sheltered the temple. Water sacred and more than ever precious. Few remaining faithful would still bathe and refresh their bodies with rancid sludgy tailings in the ghat outside. Solemnity of refused farewell. Rinsing, wringing out their thousand-year-old clothes. They came to pray to the most ancient manifestation of Shiva: Rudra, the Roarer, the Outsider, who—so tradition has it— rejected the familiar world for remote and dangerous places. Inevitably thought to build a wall enclosing the temple courtyard. Sand encroachment promptly drifted up against it. Beleaguered. Sand veiled naked copulating statues. Cups of the eyes. Dry stone eyeballs. Locks of stone hair. Carved ears sand-filled. Soft chalky look. Dulled lips' curve. Tier upon tier the swarming figures. Fretted. Stone hands open to receive divine energy, *pranha*, given whispering grit instead.

So, centuries came and went. Winds died down and gusted afresh bringing tonnes of sand to be shovelled into baskets, carted out through the gate and dumped back on the gathering dunes. Ready to come again. Endlessly hot, of course, as previously reported. Even the ghat itself dried up. In time filled with sand. Sand and more sand mounted. Restless hills rose around the temple. Hills mounded by the wind and beginning to slide down their own slopes, the unresisting and impressionable purity of silk sheets. Dry, fluid. Ungoverned beauty. Envelopment. Sand banking up against the wall began to billow over the top. The stillness of centuries and the whole courtyard buried. Stone steps obliterated. Thus worshippers trod a soft warm carpet as they stepped in.

Down there, within the stone cave of the building, priest after priest grew old. Bones sleeved in flesh. Generations of ancientness. Beads glossy with use, the white mark (e.g. on this or that forehead) the only fresh thing in the lightless windowless sanctuary. Carvings smudged and softened. The last priest-haunted shadows. Old man true to the sacred member of the god but scarcely more alive than the masks. Dwarfed wizened and exhausted. Perched on the beam of a wooden juggernaut. In bygone days young workers would drag this juggernaut out into the open. Complete with its community of minor divinities waggling at the casements and perilously perched on its squealing tower of compartments. Once were festivals of ecstasy when the same boys cast their bodies in the stone-lined street to be trampled to death. The street also gone. Enveloping forest gone, all without trace.

Just a desert temple with sand lodged in sculpted elaborations of the roof where intertwining limbs told sacred stories in limestone. Dust on limestone collarbones, in navels and under toenails. Unopposable infinity of sand. Finally throwing a sheet of itself, like the curving tide of the distant sea, in at the door. That last priest a half-blind witness. Dimly framed against the evening light (as seen from behind). No use his sweeping out what would only return at the full moon. And return. Perfect as ever. The labour of Sisyphus. Lunar dryness skittering in across the flagstones to pile its sterile tribute around the base of Shiva's lingam and fill the yoni there. Oil lamps trembled singly, no longer mirrored by a glossy floor, doomed to air by the invading carpet of granules. The worshippers, a dying breed, trudged up inclines and slithered down the other side, sand giving underfoot, into that isolated hollow in oceanic dunes. Their numbers dwindling till, at last, the lamps burnt out. Flaking curds caked the neglected lingam. Then, one night no doubt, the priest himself curled up in a corner, in among the perished trappings and ceremonial clutter of forgotten days, among bull heads and cobra masks. And never woke.

Alien silence settled. Then a thousand locusts with transparent wings. Ruby pinpoint eyes, their tiny saws akimbo. Swarmed. And left.

Following the thousand years of worship came this thousand years of sand. The temple fully buried. Nothing now but a dune, with a few knobs and finials of the roof sticking up through it. Breezes caress smooth slopes. Sunshine from clear sky. No sound. The guide book explains: 'Unlike Krishna, who departs his temple if his stone flute is ritually smashed by the priest, Shiva stays.' So, down in the dark and silence, his lingam still intact, the God himself is there. To this day.

And here they come, the new conquerors from Peoria, Crewe and Wangaratta, you name it. Stumbling out of hire cars and coaches. Doors slam. Much distinctness. Graceless flesh exhibits. Glance around like lost avengers. Apprehensive of glaring sky. Sky near the earthline egg-blue in the sand-stung wind. Call out at the tops of their voices. Absence of harmonising—e.g. feeling. Ground already slipping underfoot, they trespass. Tour guides urge them to toil up slopes. Right to the crest of the dune and down the unseen side. Unseeing, slithering sandals hampering them among shapely stones from a former age, they tread the roof of a carved cavern without the least idea. One portly man with pig's bristles. Breathless. Flips through travel agency brochure. Bellows back to warn companions coming up behind 'Not a thing! Not a single bloody thing to be seen!'

L'Étoile Bleue

Leaving San Sebastián on foot, heading north and crossing the border into France, my goal was Biarritz and the nearby village of Anglet. Battling against an Atlantic gale, I might say. I hoped to reach a youth hostel known as *L'Étoile Bleue,* famous for its friendly atmosphere and for having the best hostel food in Europe. Anyway, I was glad to put Spain behind me. With Franco still in power it had been hard. Somewhere outside Gerona some kids stoned me to chase me out of their town. I had felt helpless and ridiculous trying to run with my big pack bouncing on my back. Right across the country I was hounded, one way or another. So, with the prospect of France to encourage me, I plodded for six and a half hours through the stinging March drizzle, kept going by the promise of a fire and a hot dinner.

Finally, just on dusk, I arrived at the outskirts of the village, cold, sodden and footsore. I consulted the Youth Hostels Association handbook, drops of rain hanging off my eyebrows, found the lane in question and, at the end of it, a two-storey house with blue gables. But even a glimpse was enough to bring my hopes crashing down. The place was shut. No smoke issued from the chimneys. The shutters were closed. The garden was filled with an undisturbed scent of wet lavender. I walked up to the house and took refuge under the porch. The only sound was the patter of rain. I played the part of knocking, quite as if cameras rolled and my tragedy was being witnessed in the cinema by a sympathetic audience. Well, because I was young. What more can I say?

I knocked again, this time without acting the part. No answer. Yet I could swear that, if the house *was* empty, the last person had only just left. You know how a place can somehow feel occupied? I knocked some more, this time louder. I had rights. With my membership card ready, I checked the handbook again. There it was in print: *50 beds, open 52 weeks*. Someone had to be at home. And they were obliged to attend to my needs as a member! I unslung my rucksack and gazed back along the muddy lane winding away through slanting rain to the main road. Deepening dusk had begun gathering in purple pools among the bushes.

Hitchhikers can generally find companions on the way, but the long distance walker walks alone. And now, with night about to fall, the loneliness overwhelmed me. I only just controlled a rush of despair too childish for a twenty-three-year-old. Either I would go crazy and break in, or else break down and cry. Then I heard a window squeak somewhere above my head. Backing out from the porch and into the open, I looked up. Rain needled my face. A woman was staring down at me. The intense unseeing look she gave me fixed me to the spot. For a long moment neither of us spoke. Mutely I held the booklet open, as my explanation, my request, my proof of rights, and pointed to the *L'Étoile Bleue* entry, ridiculously, as if she could read it at that distance, rain speckles and all.

She said nothing.

And the way I saw it later in my memory she was begging me to go. She—this woman in middle age with her marvellous eyes who was (and the description I hunted for came to me only belatedly) the most beautiful woman I had ever seen—directed my way a baffled expression. Then, without a word, she shut the window.

I glimpsed her pale fingers and heard the latch click. She left me standing there. As a last resort, I tried the door handle. It gave. The way in stood open. Yet, when it came to the point, I hesitated. I thought about trespassing, lighting a fire in the stove—little chores like this were commonly expected in hostels—and making myself at home. I took a deep lungful of the cool homely smells of the place. There was nothing to be done. I had to leave, I knew that. Hating myself didn't help.

An awful empty misery ballooned in my chest as I hoisted the rucksack on my back. The damp shirt under my leather jacket squashed against me and a trickle of water found its way down past my belt. Leaving the door ajar, I don't know why, I stepped out into the rain again. Momentarily I looked back, but darkness had already begun swallowing the house and garden.

I took a bus to the nearby town of Bayonne where there was said to be a big hostel, though it was not in the official book. I peered at the passing night through steamy windows and reviewed the day: my departure from San Sebastián, the gale, the grime, a beach scattered with concrete blocks and barbed wire and craters (relics of war), my loneliness, arrival at *L'Étoile Bleue*, the upstairs window, the lady of the house with a soft loop of hair coming loose over her ears, her white fingers on the windowsill and the latch, her eyes …

At the hostel I struck up a friendship with a Dutchman by the name of Franz, a somewhat morose individual but pleasant enough. I told him about being turned away in Anglet. And he had stories of his own to tell. On and on we talked, mostly about the usual things, places we had been and places we hoped to reach, whether or not to volunteer for some community project in Africa, cars, girls and the inevitability that we would all soon die in a nuclear war. By bedtime I was in a calmer frame of mind. The next day was spent on the pillion of Franz's 900cc NSU, zooming around the foothills of the Pyrenees. That motorbike was so much fun. Life had taken another turn. I decided to stay a second night before continuing my journey by foot, north, with Lascaux as the next goal. Franz was planning to head south, so breakfast would be our last meal together.

From the top of the staircase I could see him already at the big table with a newspaper spread open before him in a patch of sunlight. As I approached he planted one finger on a headline and swivelled the page for me to read: trapped under his finger the word *Anglet* caught my attention. With only a smattering of French, I worked my way through the article. A woman's body had been discovered. Hanging from the ceiling. In an upstairs room. An upstairs front room. At a youth hostel known as *L'Étoile Bleue*. Apparently, she had balanced on a wooden stool … the hostel door was found open, so the report commented, but the house itself was in immaculate order. A fire ready laid in the grate. The lights had not yet been switched on. The footprints on the polished floor were her own. There were no suspicious circumstances. Estimated time of death: just around nightfall.

Franz stared closely at me.

My throat clogged up. I could not speak. One monstrous thought blocked my mind. Had I interrupted her? Had she, perhaps, climbed down off that stool to come to the window? My eyes swam with tears. Had she—thanks to my intrusion—had she … had I … had I put her through the agony of needing to muster the courage a second time?

A t o a s t

The stairs to the door on street level admitted a cold
slab of night air. And down into the restaurant stepped
a man immediately notable for his enormous size.
Following came a woman of much the same age, being
still in her thirties perhaps, but so stricken since birth
with a stunting illness she was no taller than a seven-
year-old. He shed his immense tent of an overcoat and
she shrugged off her tiny cape. These he hung on the
pegs provided. Then they advanced across the stone
floor among crowded tables each under its long cone of
light. Her face exactly on a level with his belt, she took
three steps on her tiny legs to each one of his. A waitress

showed them to a vaulted niche near the open fire. He did not hold the chair out for her, but with a grave smile immediately crashed down on his own. As if expecting this she hoisted herself up, little shoes dangling clear of the floor, and planted tiny elbows on the table. With hands crooked and wrists pinched by a fold of baby skin she supported her chin while gazing at the menu placed before her.

The fire burned high. Flushed with warmth they exchanged looks, as if the novelty of the place with its battleaxes and scutcheons gave them fresh eyes for each other, and talked so intimately they could not be heard at the next table. He, in his yellow woollen jumper, with his massive jaw and nose, his dense black hair and ogreish brows, rewarded what she said with the consideration of long pauses. And she, having awaited his response with the earnestness of a scholar absorbed by her research, received each word he offered as something ponderable. So, there it was again, that grave smile which now and then he excavated, lighting up his heavy features with extraordinary sweetness and grace—this time because, with some sternness, she clearly redirected his attention to the choices offered by the menu. Laughing just a little as she did so, her bosom heaving an inch above her waist. For his part, he entirely enveloped a water glass in one fist, pensive sips helping him decide. At exactly the same moment they finished with their menus, or at any rate set them aside.

Impossible to imagine how these two came to be together or what their relationship might be, that they could so completely agree on 'the mood' of the evening.

Now, so his piercing attentiveness suggested, this great bull of a man must persuade her of something. He raised one hand till he found what he wished to say, then seized the initiative in saying it. She put on a resolute demeanour and took her turn, showing animated interest, her sea-anemone fingers alive with activity to illustrate her reply. The frail gold chain she wore slipped from wrist to forearm. By way of answer, with his immense hands, he broke a hunk of bread and passed half to her. Completely unselfconscious, though perhaps hearing questions in the air, he did eventually hunch his shoulders and look up around the cellar. In doing so he seemed not so much to take account of anybody as, simply, to draw favourable conclusions from the aroma of roasted meat. A giant seated on an ordinary chair, his knees bumped the underside of the bare table when he leaned back while carefully unfolding his napkin like a piece of evidence to be considered. Tiny reflected flames danced in his eyes and on the silver blade of the knife he picked up and put back where it belonged.

So, then, she looked round too. But differently. As if somehow she had come right—and the go would never be gone out of her—as if she walked dreamily across a frozen waste only to find the frost bright, then black, and herself still feeling warm. She took account of individual faces and items of apparel and declared, by her frank interest, that she accepted company with equanimity, that she was at home among strangers and really unfussed by being the centre of attention. At last a waitress arrived to take their order and bring them wine. They returned to the confines of one another's gaze.

The deep burgundy liquid between them, their wine glasses touched in silence, each shining rim a perfect ellipse, a halo of light.

The dreaming bird

Night time in a laboratory at the University of Chicago. The building is a cube of neon brilliance afloat in the dark at the edge of the city, a tiny bathysphere of an elevator connecting the floors. Right at the top, in forty cages, birds are asleep. But the scientists observing them must stay awake to analyse the data being recorded by banks of instruments. Nothing could be more responsible. The specimens of most interest are tiny zebra finches (*Taeniopygia guttata*), notable for their white-barred black tails, natives of Australia, known to prefer nesting out in the desert or among the layers of twigs and branches at the base of an eagle's roost (daring to cohabit with such a dangerous host for the advantage of protection from lesser predators). Having developed a tolerance to water too salty for most other birds, they survive their habitat. Naturally, the laboratory caters to this saline inclination.

An electronic sensor blips for each bird, recording activity in its brain, a delicate needle trembling across the screen at the head of the telltale inscription. And right now something new takes place.

Excitement grips the scientists: one bird yields unusual results. Even while the sleeping creature lies still and silent its brain betrays specific neuron activity. The sensor already tells the story. An exact match emerges: the pattern has been recorded before. The senior woman researcher whose charge the bird is recognises this as the neuron sequence of a young zebra finch learning the song to signal the great and rare event of approaching rain: a distinctive sequence of whistles. But here and now, safe in its cage, this bird utters no actual sound—he rehearses the song in memory.

She composes her hands in her lap to prevent them trembling while fellow scientists of the Chicago University team gather round to stare, awestruck, as the needle travels its course, unravelling evidence of an instinct being transmogrified into dream.

Daniel Margoliash, chief researcher, associate professor in the Department of Organismal Biology and Anatomy, planning a press conference for the morning to explain this marvel (no doubt to journalists significantly less impassioned than himself), sketches out a few notes.

It would appear that the zebra finch, having stored the neuronal firing pattern of song production during the day, can read it out at night.

Evidence suggests the bird replays the pattern during sleep.

The specimen in question was hatched here in our laboratory, remote from—even 'dislocated from'—its native habitat.

This native habitat is in the desert.

In order for their young to survive the extremely dry conditions these birds have evolved an adjustable breeding season to coincide with the transient phenomenon of rain.

So, the pattern of song also connects to mating and the subsequent protection of newly-hatched chicks.

The rarest item in the zebra finch's vocabulary is this seldom-needed song.

The needle continues to inscribe proof of a phenomenon beyond explanation—truly a mystery: asleep in the air-conditioned lab at Chicago University, the tiny feathered creature prepares itself in readiness for rain, unaware of humans gathered round and holding their breath, it dreams the song of survival, rehearsing a memory not its own, a song it has never heard and will never use.

William Donnegan

Consider the evidence of William Donnegan's second journey north. He aimed to confirm the thunderous marvel of Niagara Falls for himself. He was, without surreptitiousness or caution, an enterprising man, a man of curiosity and intelligence. He could afford to play the tourist, this tradesman with a nose for leather, having grown rich from the boots and shoes he made—still with hard fingers and horny nails left over from when he did the work himself. That there may have been another motive for visiting Niagara, quite apart from marvelling at God's handiwork, did not diminish his grave, austere, detached awe when face to face with the irresistible natural order.

As for William Donnegan's *hopes*, well the most precious of these he had vested in his wife, a white woman, the day he married her when they were both young.

You might say theirs was a simple story, a story of black and white, a pattern of light and shadow, a photographic story, almost. Because, on that second trip north, Mr Donnegan took his beloved wife along and they travelled in style. For all this, the presence of the falls being so stupendous, he longed to make some adequate comment, to share his rapture. Body trembling with the cannonading boom of an entire river dropping off the edge—he was eighty-four, if the calendar is to be believed—an idea came to him that, at last, he had the means to communicate how his love felt, how her presence shook and overwhelmed him. But he couldn't hear himself speak. So, he took her hand and hoped that this simple gesture might raise that which he had often declared into the hymn of love he felt. In this there was nothing demanding about him in the form of a required reply. And her way of showing her contentment was to pay him no attention, having room in her mind for nothing other than the waterfall. But when next, unsmiling, she shook her head in wonder, he understood and thought that she was like a child who, hearing a bird and at the same time seeing it (as his friend Robert Fitzclarence memorably put it), cannot separate the two: taking in the sight and sound as one and the same experience. He kept this, like his quiet joy, to himself while he watched her watching that vast catastrophe of water tumultuously cascading into its own turbulence with a roar that seemed to pass beyond the realm of hearing into the pulse of a pure and universal frequency.

Yet it is true that his thoughts did wander when a drift of spray tingled against his tough old cheek. He did find himself recollecting his previous visit, three years earlier, a visit he had not mentioned to his wife because she must suspect nothing of the secret undeviating meetings held there, nor those friends and comrades dedicated to 'full political, civil and social rights for black Americans'. He had wanted to. But he was afraid the Niagara Movement might be her sticking point. Afraid she was only *all right* about his colour so long as he did not call attention to it. He had no wish to alarm her. He needed to protect his marriage and the peace he enjoyed at home. Truth to tell, as they stood together in the prickling spray, transfixed by the falls, there came a moment of lapse when the din which enveloped this unfrightenable man frightened him: the vast flow so hurtled over the precipice, as impenetrably intent as a malevolent being with the hypnotic power to draw all creation in its vortex and plunge it down into that boiling canyon of destruction. Caught in the fascination of a suicidal spasm, mid-stride, he might well have jumped ... had it not been that her warm gloved hand reached for his as if she knew.

Not long after William Donnegan returned home to Springfield, Illinois, he was amazed to hear again the unremitting noise of that great river sliding over its precipice—right there in the dreary, landlocked, peeling heart of his very own birthplace. What fantastical delusion was this? Out for his daily constitutional, the usual stroll through suburban streets, a stroll noteworthy only for the new homburg he chose to parade on this occasion (he still retained a touch of the peacock and why not?), he found himself distracted from such simple vanity by an echo of the impossible. A faint roar at first, the sound of it seeming to come slow and terrific, forever and forever, the swell that cumulatively followed announcing a catastrophe ahead. And what he soon caught sight of amounted to no less than the separation of hearing and seeing. In disbelief he found himself confronted not by a river, but by a rabble: a rabble of monotonous, self-repeating and fiercely purposeful thousands. Although several blocks away still, faces could be seen red with fury under the shadow of hats. Open mouths uttered a shameless, pent, baffled, murderous roar. And, manifested as terrifying sound, the torrent of their hatred surged his way. He recognized the rush of it as reaching back to the headwaters of the first guilty days of the slave trade.

Next thing they surrounded and jostled him, carrying him some distance before he could catch breath. It was upon them, of them, the shameless savagery. His homburg bowled into the gutter. Forced up against a shopfront by the same continuing surge he discovered the door to the place unlatched. He huddled there to wait his opportunity. So when, momentarily, the mob turned on another victim, their faces seeming to glare with bodiless suspension as if he would keep till later, his nerve did not fail; as the surge flooded back across the road and on, he twisted the handle and staggered in. The cloistral dimness a comfort, he had the presence of mind to slam the door after him and, leaning against it, shot the bolts and pulled down the blind. Only then did he realize his trespass was observed, not knowing yet how gruesome his face looked, wide-eyed and streaked with blood.

A young woman with fair hair, hardly more than a girl, cowered behind the counter. Did she think he might assault her? Would she betray him? Without a word she stood her ground with that serene, unearthly luminousness of a hospital patient under the knife. He watched her weigh the matter up. She knew what was what. Well, everyone did, after all. Then one hand rose like an automaton to check her hair with swift, trembling, practised movements. With the other she opened the door behind her and stood aside for him to go through first, even while the mob outside went howling past the shop window with the power and senselessness of an avalanche, glittering thickets of flame dancing above their heads. They dragged poor Scott Burton along with them. That's what he witnessed, too late, in the very instant of accepting her protection. Scott, his barber for twenty years, was flung down and flung up and sent staggering among a forest of legs, mob outrage booming, clear and young and too vigorous to withstand. He witnessed it, as seen past a display of jam in glass jars. This and a sudden, tremendous lick of light towering into the dusky sky. With the cry of an unassuagable fury the mob swarmed in a vortex to crowd round a tree right outside the shop. He did not need a second look. Poor Scott, nothing could save him now.

Next day the copper light still hung in the sky. Someone was said to have counted twelve thousand rioters. The violence, triggered by nothing more substantial than rumour, had needed only a trumped-up story—of some black supposed rapist being protected by a jail, any jail, where he was held—to unleash its frenzy. This he learned by the time he found his way back to his family.

Despite and still, old as he was, he survived.

So William Donnegan, cobbler, self-made man, in his way an example to his kind, reached home to be enfolded by that aged white flesh he so desired and so cherished. Her arms around him, he rested against his wife's breast, shaking with exhaustion till his anger subsided. Even then, in thick darkness, the night sky glowered with proliferating fires and bruised smoke—the whole district ablaze. Man and wife, they could not sleep for fear. Though to some degree protected by their prosperous house and its orderly garden's forbidding message to intruders, this felt like little enough. Late into the night the hubbub of too many voices did eventually dwindle and peter out to a draggle-tail of parting oaths and a residual scatter of sobs and cries. And then these were mingled with the waking call to action of those who had slept and for whom the crusade was only just beginning: a future newly opening the way ahead.

Already, in the early light, women and children posed beside the barber's dangling body for photographs as keepsakes. White families nailed fluttering handkerchiefs to their doors, like signs during an outbreak of plague, the white of exemption. For the rest ... well, too bad. Houses went up in smoke and by the time the firefighters arrived, their draught-horses clattering down echoey streets, it was too late. The entire neighbourhood burned beyond saving and the crowds moved on. But not until the second night of rioting, 15 August 1908, did the Springfield lynch mob break into William Donnegan's house. They dragged him out, clubbed him and slashed at him, cutting his throat, to teach him a lesson.

&

Nature—slow at her task, but swifter by far than the governments of men—did eventually achieve a seeming impossibility. It took another year, but in 1909 Niagara Falls froze. The roaring stopped. A vast cliff of icicles, a wall of arrested moments, towered above mounding domes and hills of snow-covered ice on which, half-blinded by sheer whiteness, enchanted sightseers in black homburg hats and black overcoats posed for the camera.

B a b a k

Whatever else she may have expected on arrival at this detention camp in the far north of South Australia the journalist did not expect Babak. Babak was thirteen years old. An asylum seeker from Afghanistan, his lips were sewn together. Crude thread zigzagged from needle-hole to bloodied needle-hole. Listening to what she had to say, he sat slumped in the dust among sixteen others, enduring a temperature upwards of forty degrees. All of them had inflamed lips bruised around the stitches. Politely they listened. Once she had finished she was told none spoke English.

An Afghan doctor, also incarcerated there, volunteered to be her interpreter.

Babak wrote down his first question for the doctor to translate: 'Do you have a city in your desert?' 'Yes,' she told him, 'but not exactly in the desert.' 'What is your city like?' And then, of course, she came up against the impossibility of describing Sydney—the heart-stopping beauty of the harbour on a sparkling day. So she invited another question instead. And it was written out for the translator: 'Who put us here?'

She thought of the Prime Minister's harbourside mansion.

Men and women edged close to hear, despite the guards in the employ of the private company administering the camp for profit. In place of an answer she invited these others to tell stories on behalf of the hunger-strikers who could not speak. The doctor did his best, listening, nodding, interpreting, finding the right words in hesitant English, bringing life to fragments of what had happened during the desperate journey to reach safety: stories of humble gatherers of wild pistachio nuts who had found the courage to defy the army—and then the insurgents—to set out on the journey. Stories of horror and repression, torture and murder, a gruelling struggle across the mountains and a long, long journey by train. Stories of the first terrifying sight of an ocean, stories of hunger and heroism and sinking vessels. And then came the account of a catastrophe of bad weather and an approaching ship, high on the horizon, headed to the rescue—men in uniform—angels, for sure.

Her interpreter produced a tattered news clipping from his pocket and unfolded it with surgeon's fingers. He gave it to her to read. Prime Minister Howard was quoted as having said: *Children in the proper, positive care of their parents don't sew their lips together, do they?* Speaking now for himself, the doctor asked what this meant. He had underlined the words: *They are trying to morally intimidate Australians.*

She had no way of explaining. Shame overcame any attempt. Her own country out there, unendingly flat beyond the razor wire, struck her as a place so strange and barren she didn't recognise it. Well, because Howard was not alone. An inescapable disgrace was already embedded in the complicit tone of the article. Babak's father, with one arm across his son's shoulders, constantly dabbed antiseptic on the boy's lips and hummed a chant. His own lips sewn and sore. There was grief in his exhausted eyes. The doctor explained that Babak had volunteered to take part in the hunger strike because he knew he would need to learn courage for when he grew to be a man with his own children to protect and feed.

From there the visitor moved on around the compound under a blazing weight of sunshine. The prison guard accompanying her explained that each detainee had been allocated a number and must be addressed by that number. This, he explained, assured them of equality. And failure to comply? He illustrated the consequences with the tale of a nursing sister who had refused to use the numbers. She had objected that such a system was tried out once before in her lifetime … by the Nazis. So, she had set about learning the patients' names. Well, naturally, the manager carpeted her and dismissed her. The guard sniffed, 'And anyway, she could never pronounce them right, from what I understand.'

Once they had completed the circuit, the journalist bid goodbye to her friend the doctor. Meanwhile Babak had written a new message: 'My mother says,' the doctor translated, 'we must be proud of our beautiful Hazara language.' She assured the boy that she had no doubt of it and that Hazaran would be beautiful again on his own lips when next he was free to speak.

'Makes you wonder,' said the guard supervising her departure, 'who they think gives a damn.'

The flame priest

Oft the old man check that flame He step outside Of death unmindful Yonden the sacred cave And still asleep Asleep he make his duty Feed with oil the clear flame think Gods thought The ritual respect We know this pride us boys One asleep boy mutter some sad thing Man voice from boy mouth Sad if woken sad with dreams With exile words his own Old asleep man greet the dawn Fox fur save him colden Priest of this day risen Some new thing here Lake-remembered fog a crust on each one twig I change me to a bat Fly big and bold out Right at that elder head While he standfast feed the flame Up then across the world The world hang top to

tail whenall I stop The wintercarish priest ask who am
I Who you are he shout while still asleep I answer I am
fire That fire that get away Him tricked he turn back in
His spirit find his body dead And friendless on the floor
He cannot breathe nor speak Back from the lake I fly
athwart his head And laugh and threat to sell him The
price of seven oxes He dead enough but wield his staff
Frost melted on his deadman hand Old deadman hot
with fury His watching lamp still drunk on oil Flamelight
spirit count us boys Me not missed nor none Growled
words of grief from one that talk Red sunspear on the
old mans chest That flame burn up So now I change me
to a fish Lakesafe underwater hearen nothing When my
friend cry out in broken voice

Winter campaign

The colossal din of an army coming to rest congests the
sky above the tundra, the crackling frosted air chock
full of noisy confusion right up to a ceiling of cloud,
everywhere boots are tramping, shuffling, stamping,
the marching mud-clogged boots of foot soldiers and a
few shiny well-heeled boots among them, everywhere
boots coming to attention belong to one category or the
other, and everywhere hands and heads, and everywhere
mouths shaped for drinking, for swearing, agape while
they issue orders or clamp tight in submission, many
gulping, others blaspheming. Detachments of assault
pioneers wield picks and shovels, hardened hands tinker

with weapons provisionally theirs to hold as long as the campaign advances from success to success and indeed runners already deliver messages pre-empting victory and all the sounds of this methodical bustle accumulate as a symphonic crescendo. Amid the hubbub of settling in, of scourings and the assemblage of mechanisms, amid preparations and repairs, with mallets tapping away at tent pegs for officers' tents behind the lines, field kitchens spouting pungent smoke, the towed artillery is trundled to new positions ready for the morning. Horses whinny as they trample their own dung. The left-right left-right of arriving rearguardsmen swells the cacophony of multitudes perpetually converging and crisscrossing the vast encampment to hold together a complex rhythm punctuated by instructions in the form of bugle calls. Eighty squadrons, comprising nine thousand four hundred and seventy-three men under arms, sort themselves out according to allotted billets. They are to bivouac in the open in groups, each group with its magazine of supplies, each with its small campfire so that, upon waking, the soldiers—having warmed their feet and slept on dried-out ground—may instantly be ready for battle. And stamped into every face (ineradicable and unmistakable, whether etched there for life or moulded of the softer stuff of momentary inspiration) is the vice that unites them, the crude bloodlust of certain victory. Preoccupied with settling their kit, cartridge box, knapsack, provisions for four days, pioneer hatchet, musket and bayonet, some among them erect straw shelters against the wind, others chance it and simply roll themselves in blankets, all with the prescient solemnity, the prescient heartbeat, the prescient tremor of unexpended adrenalin, called into being by danger, the solemn clash of arms soon to come and the expected spillage of enemy blood in combat violent enough to burn off the last reserves of energy. Meanwhile, sleep is the order of the day. Bivouacs are laid out in three lines to disguise their number by reducing the visible fires. The mood wells, bubbles up and soars: as invaders they know they are invincible and feel within them the spring wound tight, lethal energy ready to be unleashed as action, the explosive energy to tear down walls and bastions if need be, an energy uniting them with the cosmos, the striving atoms of the universe, no less, and the principle of order which holds the solar system stable in space. Tomorrow, beyond doubt, they will strike a decisive blow. Convoys of food magazines, essential apparatus of warfare, lumber up behind the army, lumber along separate roads from grain depots secured at three nearby villages, and already the first sacks of wheat for distribution have been broached and handmills begin grinding as the sun goes down, field ovens being stoked give out the mouthwatering aroma of fresh-baked bread, sutlers knock spiggots from casks hoisted on trestles for the bottling of brandy and beer. Harnesses jingle, beasts stamp the ground and drays deliver siege frames and bridge-building components. To the roar of furnaces and the wheeze of bellows armourers get busy with grindstones till an intense squealing hiss of sharpening steel escalates to mingle with the clank of heavy equipment and repairs. Metal slides against metal, timbers clock on timber, small hammers driving nails into horse hooves clunk, big hammers chime at anvils and sledge-hammers join in where the pallisades are being put up. Each pallisade surrounds an armoury of swords for the foot soldiers, carbines and bayonets, three hundred charges of powder per artillery piece, plus crates packed with ammunition and cannonballs. This is an army no nation on earth could withstand. Out at either wing of the encampment creaking carts deliver forage for the cavalry horses while, way to the rear, the groans of accident victims and those who have fallen prey to an unidentified contagion billow against the sides of a marquee hospital. Squads of mounted hussars patrol the camp, cantering out to the fringe of forest to prevent any deserters escaping. The brigadier's wolfhounds, whose food has not yet been brought, set up a frenzied barking as the setting sun finally descends into view from under a solid bank of cloud, suspended in a gash of sky, only to bloodily dissolve. Vast daggers of shadow point ahead to where, five kilometres distant, at the eastern edge of the plain, the enemy army, drawn up in ranks, camps ready to confront them at dawn, presenting itself in the distance as a strange, knotted spiderweb that extends the full width of the horizon—a smoke blanket and the sparkle of fires clearly seen to mark the contours of a ridge which is to be the defenders' sole advantage. Then the hood of night draws down on the din and a long day's march at the climax of months of preparation ends in sleep.

Sometime after dark the glass falls and keeps falling.

Cold stars thrust their way through the ceiling of cloud, fall fine as powder, and settle on the epaulettes of duty guards who shiver cheerfully. Then, quite suddenly, the massing sky crumbles altogether. Snow, in earnest, spins and spirals from a strange immeasurable remoteness, confused icy needles scratching out the last dim relics of countryside. Snow settles on blanketed bodies, on bales of straw set ready for the horses, on pointed canvas peaks of officers' tents, on the rough bark of pallisades and the smooth horizontals of cannon barrels until, densely tumbling down, it pours as a weightless cataract from the infinity of darkness, nestling softly in the manes of apprehensive horses, softly on an awning above the blacksmith's forge, softly and softer on sleeping faces, caught in moustaches and eyebrows, stealthily in the ravishing calm, settling as the embodiment of stillness. The slumbering men slumber, communing with bright secret dreams of home and sex, their collective savagery a species of innocence, while above and around them snow drifts across the tundra, impalpable as smoke, snuffing embers, erasing the dark cartridge box and knapsack at each man's head, cancelling his issue of four days' provisions, shrouding his musket, burying his hatchet, till the bivouacs, burrowed in sleep, pursue their dream under a vast white sheet. The smell of snow clots the dogs' throats. Soft flakes now sheath the metal surfaces, cushioning wood and leather, blanking out all senses, muffling touch, freezing ambition, burying the smoke and the aromas of cooking, the stench of shit and even the freshness of trodden earth, to silk ugly facts in fixity. The guns seize up, those house-sized magazines on wheels no longer stand against the sky, nor the siege-frames behind. Useless and abandoned, all are simplified, like covered furniture in a closed house where no one is expected back. With the horror-hounded lust of men sunk in the loneliness of their desires, the mineral soldiers lie scattered like sediment in a stratum of rock compacted under the glimmering mica of snowflakes innumerable beyond description. Two forty-five by the clock. Beneath the low-hanging and impenetrable sky Earth itself is luminous with a dim chill ghostly glow. Sleepwalking guards stagger at their posts, disoriented, like miners emerging from deep underground, rubbing their eyes with mittened hands, and at each blundering step their boots disappear into holes of snow. Thickening gusts of snow spinning chaotically around the sleepers mock all notion of military order, of grand strategy, of territory awaiting conquest, to diminish the land itself and swallow it in the vastness of a teeming sky, the hurtling scribble of meaninglessness. So strange and airless is the effect that the vortex sometimes seems to operate in reverse: as if the dazzle of flakes is being sucked up into the cloud cover. The snowstorm produces and reproduces itself, abating only in its own good time when a voice from the second dream whispers into this one a mysterious wordless whisper, language beyond language, to flurry, to die away, to float as an airy residue, the visible transmuted to invisibility while the drift left behind embraces, delicately, everything. And peace cradles two armies in her arms, her plumage, on her breath, mysteriously fulfilled. The sleepers sleep on, surrendered to the populated silence of dreams, dreams connecting the soul with its source, with marvels and terrors rebuilt afresh from bright untarnished child-fresh images planted long ago in each man's mind by his first encounter with rooms and family around him. Beyond the bitter end the storm passes, having expunged the last vestiges of life, the last remaining cap and shoulder. Particles still hang in a scintillant nowhere without border between earth and sky. Hours later, when the air assumes its own colour to stand motionless on the horizon, a vast smooth sickle of darkness lingers like the shadow of an approaching planet and a few belated crystals still twirl down, each one tracing its own individual helix, a stray drifting particle detached from the sky, now and then gently floating to nestle where it belongs. So destiny adds the finishing touch and the creaky light of dawn spills wonderingly to explore cloaked ground, the smooth plain, the moon-luminous earth.

The first soldier to wake, eyes cracking open, finds his comrades vanished, himself alone, surrounded by nothing—the entire army gone, all sense of direction erased—nothing to be made out on the ridge ahead, no sign of defenders, nor any objective. Seized by terror, he is islanded in the blanketing hush of the infinite.

The experiment

This is the deal, said the expert.

What is the deal? said the client.

You get encased in the product, said the expert.

But what is the product? said the client.

Do you know what that is? said the expert.

Not to my knowledge, said the client.

The expert seemed in no hurry. Finally he said: It resembles fine brown sand.

So I see, said the client.

Special stuff. Perhaps you think I'm deluded? said the expert.

Possibly but not really, said the client.

Once mixed, the texture is not unlike plaster, said the expert.

Strange smell, said the client.

Which we mould to your exact shape, packing it thickly around you while you breathe in and we invite you to hold your breath.

Then what? said the client.

Then it sets instantly to lock you absolutely still—and this is important—to seal you away.

How do I breathe? said the client.

It seals you in except for your nose. We position your nose to match a small cavity, said the expert. We have the patent.

Is it usually so small? said the client.

The cavity comes complete with air channel. No light whatsoever penetrates the curve of the channel, said the expert.

Is this the set-up? said the client.

This is the set-up, said the expert.

And neither seemed to have anything more to say for a while. If the product in particular caught the attention, it was not alone in catching it, for the coffin-like apparatus caught it too.

The terror you feel passes in a flash, said the expert after sharing the pause. Your mind will understand total helplessness for the first time.

I have known helplessness before, said the client.

You have not known helplessness like this helplessness, said the expert, because:

1. The product fills even the tiniest cracks and cavities—inside your ear, under your fingernails—in an embrace beyond anything in anyone's experience.

2. Your desperate urge to struggle will instantly leave you because in these circumstances pure reason takes over with the understanding that you must remain so until released.

3. You will know it in every fibre of your nakedness and in every sealed pore.

4. Not only will you immediately accept that no shout or scream could be heard but your jaw will be clamped shut in any case, and we have never yet heard a sound from in there, not even respiration.

5. Conserving air or energy is not an issue, for only your closed eyes and your tongue can move in that sightless silence.

6. Clients shut themselves down. They do it. We have no part in that. This is beyond instruction or education. It is even beyond warning. It happens.

7. When it happens for you the experience is going to be absolute and without precedent.

Is that all there is to it? said the client.

It is a tremendous all, said the expert.

Please explain further, said the client.

At this very moment of the process you will hear God's voice, said the expert.

God's voice? said the client.

God's voice in person, said the expert.

Can I depend on that? said the client.

Clear, present and personal. He will speak to you, said the expert. *What* He will say cannot, of course, be known to me or anyone else, or predicted.

But He will speak? said the client.

All our previous clients without exception have reported that He does and that He continues speaking with the greatest imaginable clarity, said the expert.

What about? said the client.

I've told you I cannot know but I have been told in some cases quite ordinary things.

Will I be dead by then? said the client.

Not unless we have made a dreadful error, said the expert and he laughed.

Then standing there naked the client, with bewildered laughter, joined in.

God will talk to you right up till the moment when we crack the shell with hammers and the mould falls off, said the expert.

How long will that be? said the client.

You will have no idea how long. Nor will we. We do not plan such things. We are guided by inspiration. And anyway if we were to know and if we were to tell you, it would mean nothing, said the expert.

Nothing? said the client.

Nothing. Minutes, hours, days will become bafflingly impossible for you to judge, revealing Time itself as purely molecular and indistinguishable from Being.

Outside the window it was raining. The rain rained beautifully downwards, as it always does.

You will have no idea what we are doing, or whether we even know you are still in there, the expert interrupted the silence eventually. When the moment of release happens, you will see nothing and hear nothing of its approach.

I shall be waiting for it, said the client.

You may think you will pray for escape, but no. I'm afraid the first hammer blow is going to come as a shock and the cracked shell a crisis of piercing grief, said the expert.

So, that's what I'm paying for? said the client.

It's all anyone can tell you by way of preparation,

said the expert. I've done my best.

I've to lie down inside this thing? said the client.

Give us the nod when you're ready. The product must be packed around you the instant the machine mixes it. Then the procedure can begin and you're away, said the expert and looked out through the rain-streaked window.

I will nod when I'm ready, said the client.

You are never going to be the same afterwards. Trust us, said the expert. And welcome to the God Experiment.

Gettysburg

Dear Mr Lincoln. In accordance with Departmental protocol I herewith return the draft text of your forthcoming Gettysburg speech. You propose the following words:

> *Four score and seven years ago our fathers brought forth on this continent, a new nation, conceived in Liberty, and dedicated to the proposition that all men are created equal.*
>
> *Now we are engaged in a great civil war, testing whether that nation or any nation so conceived and so dedicated, can long endure. We are met on a great*

battle-field of that war. We have come to dedicate a portion of that field as a final resting place for those who here gave their lives that that nation might live. It is altogether fitting and proper that we should do this.

But, in a larger sense, we cannot dedicate—we cannot consecrate—we cannot hallow—this ground. The brave men, living and dead, who struggled here, have consecrated it, far above our poor power to add or detract. The world will little note, nor long remember what we say here, but it can never forget what they did here. It is for us the living, rather, to be dedicated here to the unfinished work which they who fought here have thus far so nobly advanced. It is rather for us to be here dedicated to the great task remaining before us—that from these honored dead we take increased devotion to that cause for which they gave the last full measure of devotion—that we here highly resolve that these dead shall not have died in vain—that this nation, under God, shall have a new birth of freedom—that that government of the people, by the people, for the people, shall not perish from the Earth.

This text has now been examined and found to contain numerous infringements of intellectual property rights. The holders of these rights insist on their ownership under sanction of the law. You are required, therefore, to respect these rights of property and, unless terms have been negotiated with the proprietors, to delete all reference to the following to avoid infringement of rights. Four Score (a gambling software program licensed by the Macrosoft Corporation), Nation (a weekly political journal), Liberty (fabric design label), The Proposition (a chain of strip clubs), Created Equal (war-of-the-sexes appliances marketing), Civil War (denim clothing), Endure (deodorant), Battle-field (depilation services and chest waxing for men), War (lipstick), Final Resting Place (multi-level cemetery opportunities), Live (Korean cellular phone), Fitting and Proper (school uniform underwear), 'Cannot' (slogan of the Untimate Strict Diet Campaign), The Brave Men (association of single fathers), Living and Dead (lost persons search agency), Power to Add (calculators and pocket organizers), Little Note (post-it tabs), Never Forget (perfume), Unfinished Work (bankruptcy inducement strategies), Thus Far (pregnancy interventions), Nobly Advanced (brassieres), 'For us to be here' (cover song), The Great Task (mobile garbage-compacting services), Honored Dead (rock band), Increased Devotion (slow-release testosterone boost capsules), Full Measure (Short-cut Mathematics for Intermediate and Advanced Students),

Resolve (lemon-charged washing powder), Died in Vain (campaign against animal fur products), Under God (sexual positions for Tantric exponents), A New Birth of Freedom (euthanasia pills), Government of the People (restraints, halters, whips and handcuffs), People (social sciences newsletter), Perish (cockroach poison), Earth (perfume-free allergenic soap).

We are pleased to advise that, in the absence of negotiated terms, the text for your speech is approved as follows:

and seven years ago our fathers brought forth on this continent, a new   , conceived in   , and dedicated to   that all men are   .

Now we are engaged in a great   , testing whether that   or any   so conceived and so dedicated, can long   . We are met on a great   of that   . We have come to dedicate a portion of that field as a   for those who here gave their lives that   might   . It is altogether   that we should do this.

But, in a larger sense, we   dedicate—we   consecrate—we   hallow—this ground.   who struggled here, have consecrated it, far above our poor   or detract. The world will   , nor long remember what we say here, but it can   what they did here. It is for us the living, rather, to be dedicated here to the   which they who fought here have so   . It is rather   dedicated to   remaining before us—that from these   we take   to that cause for which they gave the last   of devotion—that we here highly   that these dead shall not have   —that this   ,   , shall have   —that that   , by the   , for the   , shall not   from the   .

Yours faithfully.

A couple

In middle age Ms Arabella Tomlinson and the former Mrs Mackenzie (that is to say, Mavis Mackenzie) sought refuge with each other. Mrs Mackenzie had suffered thirty years' marriage to Mr Mackenzie (Alfred, of unlamented memory). She left him before he died, so she was able to tell him what she thought of him ... not that this could be claimed as a great enough triumph to have actually caused his heart attack. A pity, that. No, he lasted, in his swinish alcoholism, another five years. Indeed it was precisely this five years of separation which became so bitter a torment to his escaped wife that she took refuge with a lover—her needs and so forth—things being as they were for a woman alone ... the cost of living going up the while, plus inevitably spending a fortune at the pharmacy.

The lover, Arabella Tomlinson, a woman of her own age and inclinations who declared herself as 'never known to say a thing I had to take back', clasped Mrs Mackenzie—Mavis, Mavis!—to the warmest of bosoms, called her Pussycat and titillated her with sexual pleasures she had never imagined possible. Nay, flushed with these delights they decided to go the full hog and pool their meagre savings. They bought a tiny house on the time payment plan, though it cost lots more than they could afford, a tiny garden to dig and a tiny terrier to help them dig it (which, composedly, the obliging animal set out to do without delay). Now this ... this, Arabella declared, looking around after they moved in and she could safely shut the door on her prize, this is civilised!

To do justice to brave misguided humanity, I admit they were happy for a while.

But, alas, the delights proved ephemeral. I wish I could tell you otherwise, but things got in the way. Trouble being that they both had standards. Among the thousand hazards of intimacy these two ladies fell victim to all but very few. Sudden ferocities revealed themselves in the shape of the right way to fold a towel, the appropriate tightness for the kitchen tap. Wilful little acts of tenderness grew rare, perfect love revealed itself as something less than the anticipated bed of roses and the mask of pleasure fell away to reveal tyrannical jealousies.

Then there were Mavis's sons (twenty-nine, twenty-seven and twenty-four) who, feeling themselves unable to handle the situation in a scientific spirit, unanimously and publicly let it be known that they regarded her coming out as disgusting, as undermining their respectability, exposing them to ridicule, costing them friendships—and, worse, promotion—and, as if these indignities were not enough, retrospectively soiling even their birth with the taint of an unnatural perversion. In other words there could be no appealing to *them* for rescue from Arabella, as they made clearer than clear, not on your (adj.) nelly! Mavis took to gazing morosely into her purse as if to find there the cause of depletion which, as she very well knew, was her share of paying off the house, meanwhile hoping to God something awful would happen in the world to restore her sense of proportion, some tragedy on an international scale to overshadow her suspicions and make her feel better.

Arabella herself had only ever preferred women, she being of a more determined and focused character, besides being less compromised by conscience. She, likewise, had nobody to turn to, her previous 'adventure' having been unmasked as 'a vicious little slut after all', there was no going back. The upshot was that, with little else to do—stranded in a manner of speaking—both ladies, stuck with reciprocal bad luck, and committed besides to an ambitious confidence in victory, took up the same retirement hobby of systematic investigation: spying on each other.

Nothing went unnoticed. The little house became a mine of evidence. Unfamiliar numbers listed on the monthly telephone bill, postmarks compromising the mail, footprints across a garden bed, their little car's fuel gauge unaccountably down to empty, a knife left on the bench top ... every such detail was examined for clues and, in all fairness, the general putting of this and that together *did* seem to yield giveaway signs. A gap in the curtains suggested an overture, a signal to some third party lurking outdoors and just waiting till the coast was clear. A stray undergarment, not noticed when the wash was being put in the little machine they'd chosen with such enthusiasm, took on the status of a temptation set aside for some unnamed nose to sniff in private (the undies, of course, not the washing machine). Neglected taps dripped. Dead lightbulbs occupied a growing number of sockets. The house cleaning went to pot as a strategy of war. You know how it goes. Galloping aggravations. The roof leaked. The stairs grew treacherous. There were even, now and again, actual traces of interlopers as-yet-unknown. So, when seated either side of their kitchen table, united by the odour of infusing teabags, eyes apparently closed against each other, the ladies watched through expertly narrowed slits to detect the minutest adjustment in the other's body language ... the least telltale rustle of fabric might indicate discomfort due to some minor and, of course, secret triumph. Oh, such gloating!

You ask about the dog? Well, that bewildered little dog grew tinier than ever, finding itself enlisted as assistant investigator on both sides and confronted on a daily basis with the agony of choosing between rival enticements as the ladies competed for its loyalty. When the dog died it was just them, each rousing her mind to review a retrospect of betrayals too numerous to count but none of them slight enough to be let go.

Sad to say, the story had no end. The pattern was set. There was no way out. With their skills thus refined Mavis and Arabella proved, to a remarkable degree, equally tenacious till they only ever heard each other's voice by eavesdropping on phone calls (calls being made, no doubt, to or by conspirators of one complexion or the other). So, they reached the consummation of their passion in hatred—hatred measured out by the scruple—filling each other's lives with unasked-for assistance, wordless unwanted services and mute courtesies as venomous as they were delicate.

Sunken liner

Divers guide their deep-sea bell to swoop down through the green shafted gloom of a netherworld as ancient as the planet to prove that death can have its compensations which had never been thought proveable, for among them death has always been accepted as final and without value, they being scientists who keep their superstitions secret and rely on the material world as the repository of all things precious and a definition such as it may be of eternity. So down they go this day in their innocence to dispel a commonplace mystery deep among plants of an underwater forest, their searchlight stabbing diagonal flashes among towering trunks until on the ocean floor they discover the message they seek, the bold calligraphic curve of a hull inscribed in mud, the long-bladed keel a declaration of disaster, ranks of wafered decks tipped on one side and the cylinders of defunct funnels all colossal, all motionless. Blind to the myriad griefs which hang innumerable and suspended like so many exhausted fireflies they cross her stern which bears the name *CELESTIA* in letters taller than the tallest man to glide into the vast shadowy vagueness of a ghost ship sunk in ruin, a gaping hole in the hull revealing glimpses of the engine room with massive sludge-embedded pistons till farther round the sheer steel cliff they find themselves peering in through portholes bearded with weeds, transported back to the grand days of sea travel when escape from pursuit seemed possible. All around the wreck giant stems tower three hundred metres up to an undulant crown of foliage protected from air by a thin sheath of waves, stems as vertical and chain-like as some category of computer built on repetitious parallels, some cuneiform abacus secreting solutions to the origins of matter, some giant brain which might eventually crack the code of our prodigious ignorance of a shitty destiny. The new arrivals scan a fungus-grown honeycomb of drowned decks where passengers once strolled and sought to mask disquiet at the fate of family and friends by chatting sociably, the diving bell homes in on the head of a companionway and following once-brass rails down into the belly of the vessel its pencil of light spills along a line of fallen-open doors where tipped-up bunks prompt investigation, the capsized chairs and exhibits of such necessary junk as mirrors safety-razors quilts and cushions of mud and keys to doors forever shut against the owners' return and clocks with mechanisms set going in 1936, tools and trinkets and wind-up gramophones and a shellac disc of Caruso singing about sunshine *O Sole Mio* as he first sang it all those years ago into the ear of a recording horn—a tumbled museum of neighbourliness in the mementos of the disinherited whose belief in the future was buried along with their latched trunks of folded clothes and books of Mosaic law so deep that only the most tremendous shifts of current could cause the least disturbance, lured as these refugees had been by the promise of freedom to live according to their beliefs and a blind eye turned to the objection that some such journeys in search of justice involve displacing the least fortunate of those already there—thus the deep sea bell with its single probing beam tracks along riveted steel plates and the folded-aside flaps to kitchens where domed burial mounds of pots and bowls were left in stillness by the doomed crew scrambling for survival. Subsequently they float up the other companionway to reach the First Class decks again and the light lances in across public saloons which were once noisy with predictions of a cataclysm disastrous enough to overwhelm Europe even as the ship itself was overwhelmed by the ocean and so suddenly drowned that the whole company went down with their dreams unspoiled and their misgivings about the life awaiting them in cities built by the convict labour of an earlier time intact and uncorrupted by knowledge of what was to come: the utter strangeness of civilised men being able to stomach their own bestiality even while consigning children to experiments that rats were not sufficiently evolved to satisfy, of the self-styled master race flaying human bodies for lampshade skin. So at least those who perished aboard *Celestia* did so in the dignity of ignorance, with their belief in redemption embalmed as was their meagre baggage of necessities in the last enveloping echo of an uproar and a plunge to the bottom, their prayers bottled up in the air vents and their cries for help preserved in brine, while whales sailed overhead unstoppable as clouds among membranous strands of plankton. And, strange to report, these scientists in their deep-sea bell, even now abandoning such systematic investigation as they've begun, as if feeling themselves intruders, intentionally float straight past the bridge from the era of horizons encrusted by living growths, float away among the shadows of a giant brain active with attendant fish, a dislodged manta ray having revisited the rumour of blood feasts in the stillness of decayed light sent winging out from the wreck among the trunks of that fairytale sea forest, and they float up escaping the cosmic cold ceaselessly tucked around unused lifeboats returning without explanation to the surface to confirm that the disappearance was a mystery and the *Celestia* lost without trace having left no message to shame the world when she went down.

The Beefsteak Room

The actual invitation when delivered was perhaps only a
shade less surprising than the event itself, which followed
a week later. In brief, Alice, Sir Richard Burton's wife,
and Sir Richard himself—adventurer, explorer and
translator of *The Arabian Nights* in sixteen volumes—
were invited to dine at the Beefsteak Room, by Abraham
Stoker of all people. Their host, poised ready as he was to
claim celebrity in his own right as Bram Stoker, creator
of Count Dracula, met them at the restaurant door with
some ceremony, winsomely and with a certain bashful
self-assurance seeing them settled in their appointed
seats. That they might have harboured reservations about

the bother of walking abroad and appearing in public for the sake of *noblesse oblige* was now beside the point. Plainly they were determined to make the best of what could turn out to be a pleasant enough occasion after all.

Certain it is, at any rate, that the evening got off to an acceptable start, their host's deference remarkably in accord with the Burtons' opinion of themselves. Indeed, rather more charmed than either seemed likely to admit, their conversation began casually and personally, even to the degree that Sir Richard did not react against a sly mention of his imminent retirement from the diplomatic service, a retirement which public opinion and elementary politeness ought surely to have avoided as too ticklish a matter for a new acquaintance to raise. He, Sir Richard, in fact took quite the opposite view— not only because he had 'had enough' of diplomacy but because vengefully he looked forward to the prospect of abandoning his detractors and colleagues alike to manage as best they could without him, for the world in general conceded that though difficult and short-tempered he was nevertheless indispensable, with comprehensive experience of the entire region from Arabia to Afghanistan, experience garnered with the aid of a phenomenal mastery of twenty-five languages which he had put at the service of the British Empire.

Mr Stoker being Irish born had quite other loyalties and his slyness was not to be lightly brushed aside. He was besides even more consumed by an appetite for heroics than for the splendid dinner he had provided. The initial pleasantries being soon exhausted he pulled himself then at last together for the purpose of steering talk to the larger and less easily defended territory of the past in general. Behind his mild smile the fellow was on his mettle and gratified to find himself not at all shaken now he had fairly set the plan in motion. Next with disarming frankness he confessed that his family tendency to repeat anecdotes had become accepted among friends as a cross to be borne, as the price of friendship, a friendship, so he hoped but could not for reasons of modesty affirm, in many respects generous and sincere.

'Though, of course, *you* are the master storyteller,' he insisted and appeared convincingly humble. Then with the air of a man not wishing to be thought a mere flatterer he justified this claim, surprising Sir Richard with mention of a similar dinner party at the same restaurant many years earlier, '… a dinner party at which you are rumoured to have enthralled the company with an account of how, as a young man, you joined a pilgrimage to Mecca disguised in Arab clothing, wasn't it!'

It was beautifully expressive, the way their own silence made the murmurous surrounding conversations seem doubled in volume. At the clatter of many knives and forks, Stoker himself turning somewhat away from the table lamp to shield his face in shadow, the prospect of the evening before them darkened. To both the Burtons some unwritten contract had been in different ways breached as this *faux pas* seemed strategically predicated on common report that the great man never refused a challenge.

'What's that to you?' Sir Richard snapped coldly, thrusting his face across the crystal and silverware closer than conventional good manners allowed.

Promptly a cluster of waiters arrived in a show of efficiency to clear away soup bowls stained with delicate tidemarks of consommé. Their intervention granted Lady Burton her chance to thwart the looming conflict so, colouring, she gave Stoker wild-eyed, wavering signals. It was one of those moments at which she had, in her extraordinary way, most the air of designedly siding with her husband in order to rob him of his massive forcefulness.

'Well, my dear, everyone does remember! Everyone!' she hazarded in the hope that her placatory impulse might avoid detection and that with the intuitive flair for which she was notorious in her own circle if not her husband's she might restore the prospect of a pleasant but innocuous evening—also for no better reason than that she was slower than Sir Richard to take a dislike to their host, in whom however she began to sense a curious, perhaps unhealthy, fascination for Burton's violent nature. Having both men turn their attention her way she took it up again more soothingly and, as it were, to close the matter: '*Everyone* remembers, you goose. Everyone admires you.'

'What seems to have been so much remarked by your admirers,' the intrepid Irishman seized on her word, to all appearances unaware of his blunder and as if helping cover her unguarded 'goose', 'was the desperate and exciting aspects of the climax rather than the arduous length of the journey you undertook. Although for the whole of that journey you maintained your disguise as a pilgrim, if I'm not mistaken. Weren't you said to be the first European to gain entry to the holy city, birthplace of Muhammed? ... the first Infidel to enter the *al Haram* mosque? ... to see the *Kaaba*, I declare to God! ... the risk, man!'

Sir Richard Burton leant back and took his time sampling a swig of claret before setting his glass down with deliberation and, as waiters scooped breadcrumbs from the cloth with silver trenchers, shook the remnant folds from his napkin with a brief and decisive whipcrack. 'Have you quite finished?'

Most men would have backed down but with his robust reasonableness Abraham Stoker was not so easily dissuaded, nor were his motives either open or transparent. That indeed he had now, almost gaily, further implications to pursue, was revealed as tactical forethought in having chosen a venue so very crowded. 'No, by God,' he declared, 'you are too reticent altogether. That fascinating story of yours, so I'm led to understand, held the entire company spellbound.' He wagged a finger with the friendliest familiarity and sniggered soundlessly. 'You did survive, after all ... despite the fact that the least failure of nerve would most likely have revealed the deception, called attention to your disguise, your false identity *n'est pas* ... even the slightest hesitancy—surely?—in the subtle observances of that creed, I mean ... and then the climax, sir! The climax!'

Again the establishment's waiters interrupted to surround the table with the business of serving whole plaice, incidentally blocking the curious glances directed that way. Sir Richard growled at the plate set before him as the babble subsided to a murmur and he growled again at the apportioning of butter sauce while his wife went public, casting resentful glances from one corner of the room to another. 'Really!' she objected sharply.

'… the slightest hesitancy would have aroused suspicion, I suppose, at such a time,' Stoker mused on, meanwhile running his fish-knife down the spine of the poached creature on his plate, 'so you risked actual death, was it? … which is to say, supposing we are to believe the rumour …'

'What are you hinting, man?' Sir Richard barked. 'That a tiny lapse escaped me?'

Lady Burton clashed her wineglasses together with a blundering hand now the challenge exposed them more humiliatingly than ever to the curiosity of even the most phlegmatic diner. She was in her husband's interest, naturally, and it fully came up in her determination *not* to countenance further talk of his adventures. Nonetheless she suffered a spasm of resentment at her sensation of being empty of interest on her own account. The moral, as she well knew, of course, being that the more one gave oneself the less of one was left. So be it. But Abraham Stoker, despite the loophole her contrived clumsiness offered him, his expression betraying in roughly equal measure both the enthusiasm of the hunter and the fear of the hunted, kept the subject alive.

'… a momentary,' he prompted, 'failure.'

'Failure?' the great man thundered, his black brows drawn together and his black moustache bristling. 'Or are you perhaps suggesting loss of nerve?' He slashed at his fish, splitting its frail white flesh and propelling a glazed wafer of lemon across the tablecloth. 'Could you concede *loss of nerve*?'

'Or loss of nerve, for sure,' Stoker agreed affably. 'As you yourself just said … a lapse, as such. Granted great courage, a lapse brief as the flicker of an eye.'

The Beefsteak Room, redolent already of cigar smoke, paused in the tremendous interest of someone's having, of *his* having, at last fired a direct shot. Yet nowhere could have so asserted its British opposition to the luxury of foreignness, the indulgence of harbouring the least sympathy for—let alone respect paid to—Islam, for example. It fully came up for the assembled company then that the longueurs of dinner were to be enlivened by the relief of someone pulling down the roof on their heads.

Sir Richard Burton, not a man to waste energy in sentimental regard for his neighbours, least of all where their polite affectations were concerned, bellowed, 'What of it? Let me repeat the story, just in case there is anyone, anyone within earshot, who has not yet heard! I did travel in disguise to Mecca with a caravan of the faithful. And there came a point when I realized one young man had taken particular notice of me. In that instant of silence I knew he had seen through my disguise. And when he then stole away into the shadows, naturally I went after him, though in such a way as not to awaken the suspicion of the others.'

'You stuck a knife into his heart,' the incorrigible Lady Burton shrieked.

It had made him, this ancient peril, what he became as a diplomat, and the remembrance was not easy; it had taken its toll for, ill-advised though he might be thought, he was not cruel. Well, anyone there to witness, while hesitating over their own meal, could judge the pride of his confidence. And although, in what he next said, the great man's tone baffled interpretation, it resounded penetratingly enough despite being quietly spoken.

'As one hears you have literary pretensions,' he remarked with the calm of pantherish energy, addressing the air above Abraham Stoker's head, 'I wonder do you share my enthusiasm for *The Portrait of a Lady*?'

The surprise was less that he so abruptly steered conversation in this harmless direction than that he had left the attempt so late: this high, distinguished, polished, unrepentant reprobate who viewed history itself from a personal eminence was now fully in control of his voice. But his host was too far gone in envy.

''Tis said to be a fact, too,' Stoker persisted, even while drawing back as if *he* might be next to find a knife in his ribs, 'on the occasion when you yourself recounted this remarkable story, that several dinner guests stood up. They left the restaurant in protest, did they not?'

'Are you about to imitate them?'

'Not at all—and, by the way, I abhor Henry James's book—I merely ask. The truth fascinates me. It's a failing of my nation. So, in short, an Arab boy paid with his life for you to preserve your deceit?'

Sir Richard Burton extracted a fish bone from between his teeth and took a good look at it.

'Perfectly true, he did.'

The customary bustle of the Beefsteak Room having long since fallen quiet, waiters hesitated, mid-step, with balanced dishes. How the diners saw what they saw and heard what they heard, let alone what scandal they attached to the scene, none followed the example of those former witnesses by offering to surrender the pleasures of dinner in favour of moral indignation. Even Mr Stoker seemed now struck by the fact, sufficiently plain, that he might need to be careful of any further lapse in good manners. The danger was vividly before him and the protections of the room insufficient. As he held his tongue the restaurant fairly glowed with little lamps.

'It has never troubled me,' the great man then added in a bright, deep voice; meeting his questioner's eyes with a savage stare in which some kind of invitation seemed to lurk, 'from that day to this.' (When Bram Stoker came to chronicle this confrontation he added a typical flourish of his own: *As he spoke the upper lip rose and his canine tooth showed its full length like the gleam of a dagger.*)

Lady Burton, having had quite enough of such brief but thorny complications and well used to young men being mesmerized by her husband's elegantly brutal charm, again resorted to judicious clumsiness, pushing her plate away so sharply it knocked against the cruet. The sound of it punctuated the hush like a tiny bell.

'To kill a man, so I understand,' she concluded neutrally, grimly, as a verdict arrived at by fine, cold commonsense, albeit with the finality of a theatrical loftiness that fell just short, 'as long as it is over *there* … in the desert, I mean … is a small matter apparently.'

Querencia

There comes a moment of stillness in the bull ring when the tormented beast must face death without knowing what death is. Yet the *moment*, as such, is clearly a different matter: the moment rich with solemnity is already in its blood, as is knowledge of rare startling encounters with things not expected. Stillness descends, completing the climax of a ceremonial Dance of Death prefiguring the eternal silence, a Dance of Death played out among men in gorgeous costumes. At the epicentre the matador leans in, overshadowing the beast's lowered head, sword poised steady, the tip an inch away from the great mound of shoulder and at an angle perfect for puncturing the lung. The last flutter of movement dies away, lulled. The hush—*querencía* the Spanish call it—is a unison of the collective spirit. Even squalling babies, sensing some profound arrival, pause for breath.

On one particular day each year, in Valencia, a special category of bullfight offers rising young stars of the *corrida* the chance to swap places with their mentors, who must serve them as picadors. A raucous crowd gathers on the tiered benches for this preview of up-and-coming talent. And I am here. A band, as usual, blares execrably throughout the general posturing and parading, the bass drum sounding like wet cloth. Thirty children shuffle out, all playing accordions more or less in unison. Across the sandy arena horsemen shuttle this way and that. One rider doffs his feathered black hat while proceeding towards the fence to shake hands with the president. Two policemen smoking cigars engage in an amicable but obstinate dispute. A sign-carrier steps out into the open—he holds up a placard and revolves it for all to read:

> *No 1: S. Domecq.*

This voiceless announcement is walked the full lap. Then the youth himself puts in an appearance, acknowledging a burst of applause. He seems too much a boy to be allowed in so dangerous a place. Especially because, with no further warning, a bugle call announces the bull and the danger charges straight at him. He steps aside at the last possible moment as the bull thunders past, across the arena, and slews round at the far side to assess what's new: trots a little and props again—barrel-bodied, with a broad back, wicked horns and big staring eyes—the embodiment of now. But also, so it turns out, the signal for methodical torments to be applied. Picks are planted in the animal's shoulders and left there skewered in flesh, shafts dangling and flopping. Then the horsemen withdraw for those on foot to baffle the bull with flapping capes before dodging out of sight behind the barrier. The first flurry passes.

Now, at last, the maddened creature can fix on a single enemy.

Young Domecq squares to the menace, coolly executing a pass. This is well done, but seems not enough for him: in a gesture of bravado he casts his hat aside, sending it skimming across the gravel, and fully spreads his arms to offer his heart. Ah, yes! Bravado is exactly what the crowd is here for! In pass after pass he works closer and closer till he and the bull circle, tight enough to actually brush against one another, the monster hip-nudging him like an irate relative. He even goes down on one knee, his nonchalance is impressive and his timing seems perfect till a scything horn whips aside the curtain of the cape and grazes his armpit. He clutches at the injury and springs to his feet, moving fast. The bull moves fast too, veers about and paws the ground. The boy glides forward, plainly elated, like a musician aloft on his own virtuosity but, by further mischance, loses a slipper. Without even looking down he kicks the other off too. The homely tenderness of stockinged feet unleashes a tidal wave of sympathy around the full circle of the stadium. Hatless and shoeless, somehow supremely vulnerable, the rising star now turns his back on the bull, even as it charges him. Though gifted with neither good looks nor height, by his decisiveness and style and unflinching courage— drawing out each successive manoeuvre, as if slowing time itself—he brings the crowd to its feet.

This is what we came for.

Thus, S. Domecq controls the stillness and holds it to his purpose. No one dares breathe. Bull and bullfighter: the tableau embodies a brutal inevitability, a ceremony of farmlands and the breeding of herds, of bloodlines and an ancient nobility, symbolic of human pre-eminence in the hierarchy of God's creation. Time is suspended, the first *querencía* of the afternoon has been a spellbinding success. There is admiration, too, for the fierce and gallant bull as, with a single thrust, the young man buries his sword to the hilt and steps clear. The vanquished beast wavers—knowing death now— collapses on its knees and rolls over.

The stadium goes mad. Fans throw hats, shoes and handkerchiefs, flowers, leather wine flasks and even handbags as the victor retrieves his slippers, shrugs at the humble effort of scuffing his feet into them, and sets out to parade around the arena, bare-headed, even now obeying some sensible instinct not to strut. The whole town adores him already. His future is made. Meanwhile, sturdy horses dragging the carcass off leave behind them a sweeping brushstroke of bloodied sand.

The turn of another budding matador has come.

Players in the masque of death reassemble, their pink-and-gold capes open like flowers for the new man of the moment to confront his destiny. This fellow, by contrast, has natural elegance. It also seems he has acquired a name to live up to. He plays the part to perfection. He displays himself and then retires for a few minutes behind the barrier till the preliminaries are complete. The bull, a liver-coloured brute, is let loose. Capes fan out here and there around the arena. The angry confused bull charges hither and back, kicking up spurts of sand while picks, duly planted in those bunching shoulders, bounce and tear the flesh. One horse, driven against the barrier, is saved only by its thick leather armour skirt and the evasive skills of a quick-thinking rider. Finally maddened and at bay the bull lowers its head, seeking an enemy willing to stand. All is in readiness for the young star. He advances with red cape and sword. We applaud. This will be good. The bull goes for him. He brings off a pass. But the tiniest hint of faltering mars his style. And that massive antagonist is wild and quick, skidding into a turn to hurtle back at him. The young man hastily leaps to one side. Nimble though he is his dignity suffers and his hat slips crooked. Again the bull is upon him. Picadors move in, tense now and ready for an emergency.

Suddenly an ugly mood grips the crowd, a mixture of anxiety and contempt, as the confrontation unravels. And even when the apprentice matador survives a sequence of close shaves and succeeds in working his quarry to a standstill, preparing to deliver the *coup de grâce*, there is a stir of disapproval—this animal has not been brought fully to its moment. The best that can be hoped for now is that the ritual will be dispatched swiftly to have it over and done with. In plunges the bright sword—misplaced—buried deep in wounded muscle but missing the lung. Blood gushes out across the beast's withers. The sword stuck there in its flesh, the bull, hurt and dangerous, hurls itself blindly at the enemy. Disarmed, the young man abandons his polished bearing to skip out of the way. Colossally the animal braces to fling itself right-about. Experienced fighters close in on the combat zone, circling, alert and wary. They will only intervene for the sake of saving life. Their very concentration is a mark of disdain. Ostracised and already with no future, the youth paces this way and that, swordless, distracted, shamed and desperate. Bent forward at the waist, handsome face drawn, cape trailing and arms crooked helplessly, his body awkward and callow, he reveals how very young he is. Hating the bull, he hates himself as well. The gorgeous purple and gold costume and pink stockings look ridiculous.

Ritual broken, the dance becomes a shambles. Butchers in fancy dress gyrate around an exhausted victim. The beast's own cape—this time living blood—swathes its neck. Its tongue protrudes in distress. Yet the horns are dangerous still. Once more the young man backs off. He must retrieve his sword to attempt another, better-placed lunge, but dares not reach to grasp the gilded hilt. The veteran bullfighters gather close around to talk him through the crisis: this exchange of words the last break with ceremony and the most mortifying surrender of all. Plainly, he does his best to act on their advice. He tries. He reaches for his sword. But those deadly horns are still between him and success. Though he is quite tall, the stretch requires him to move right up against the quarry. He wavers. He cannot do it. The mentors try to rescue him from cowardice (or what we foreigners might call good sense) while the stricken bull, cornered and bewildered, eyes them off with a sliding sideways malevolence.

There is no word for loneliness, only a clumsy approximation. He stands marooned, somehow as if no longer there, like a fragment of memory. The heart knows the cold home and desperate abandonment of the gravel he stands on. He is in hell. And no one cares, which is part of it.

A pole is brought, a pole with a hook at one end. The crowd groans when the young man accepts this implement. Positioning the hook with a carefulness that is itself humbling, he yanks his sword free. Here and there spectators laugh. The bull staggers. Even now the matador cannot seem to decide quite where to plunge it for a second try. But, finally, he stabs it in ... more or less fatally. There is no *querencía*. The bull slumps to the ground, roaring for breath—belatedly, protractedly and hideously dying.

Picadors stand round in casual attitudes while the hero of the moment has no choice but to step up and bow to the president (who barely acknowledges his existence) and to the patrons. They do not waste applause on him, already busily burrowing among snacks and attending to the demands of the brats they've brought along to see a thing or two—one of whom turns round and sticks her tongue out at me.

M o d e s t y

Things reached such a pass that Emma caught herself thinking. Everyone knows that thinking is not just thoughts. Why should thinking make anyone sad. But it did and it had. And she did. And there were no visitors. She lived with her father and that was why naturally. But perhaps not.

Emma had caught herself thinking not of her father but thinking of him. Of him at all hours invariably. Morning or night she had a sense that she had no right. Yet she thought. And everyone knows what everyone knows. Do you see what I mean. His young man's whiskers his crisp whiskers were his and emerged on her despite her scruples. Just as the fact emerged more and more clearly that he might be her last chance of marriage. And marriage was very much the thing. The only thing.

At any rate she was soon sick with it and spent her time lying on a chair. Sick because the impossible was so very nearly possible. Listen closely. He was her cousin, so the barrier of strangeness was no problem. And she knew him, so the barrier of shyness was no problem either. It must not be forgotten that she was a year senior. It must not be forgotten that she had the advantage she had talked down to him. Do you see what I mean, she had bossed him about when they both were little.

The asphyxia brought on by her thirtieth birthday could and might be escaped. And if there are more ways that is one thing but she only saw this way. She was like that. And he was her only cousin who would do. Except that now he had taken it into his head to become ambitious. He had gone away after all.

The things we are seeing here! The lake, the goldmine, the animals! At our first glimpse of the lake we saw the celebrated floating islands. They are everywhere, composed of the broken off stalks of dead plants that get meshed together and compacted. Many are quite huge. The wind blows them so they sail with the stateliest

slowness from one side of the lake to the other, in some
cases with cattle or horses standing on top as passengers.

It is not of the smallest importance what he actually saw.
What was important was what he meant. I wish to say
all I know about the scientist's cousin and her hopes.
Because in this way a woman ages sooner as she did not
care to die. Those who marry when they marry young
are necessarily younger than their husbands who are
older and very often not only older but twice as much
older. So you could say he was twice as much younger.
And where did this leave her. He was to have been a
success after all.

It is painful to know of disadvantage and not know
if others have declined to notice or only pretend.

Leave her and believe her. Could she take the
factual enthusiasms of his reply to her letter to mean.
Did they mean he had not seen through her reasons. This
surprised her. There are many kinds of surprise. Not all of
them pleasant. This surprise was simple. But of course it
was foolish to think such things. He was a year younger
when they were children and it mattered. And now it
mattered more with being boosted by her hope on his
account. The year difference made no difference now
except the worst difference of all.

So there they were, the cousin and the cousin.

She did not know if he had indeed failed to suspect her strategy, well no not at all except and insofar as her intention might be welcome as she intended oh always intended. Thinking made her sad. She is putting everything away and taking everything out every day. She was just in the garden while her father got richer and owned and owned and she lived with him but she lived alone.

Well the news she received from Santiago was not what she anticipated anxious for breath, if you wish, and never had been other than puzzling. His reasons for writing remained obscure because he was really not what he should have been. So perhaps her motive had been detected. Perhaps not. Her letters were secretly tender. This came about quite naturally. It is foolish to think that at thirty a young woman is perhaps not young enough. In a way it does not matter even what is said. And now to tell and to tell very well perhaps she is shamefaced in her dignified way. And quietly screaming. Because she has experience of so very few flirtations. She justifies herself to herself as having had so little practice.

Once upon a time when she was still too young to be on guard there had been a young man. Of course there was because this is the way of young men. It is the way of young men to be there. Listen to her story. He was a soldier and beautiful in his grenadier's courage and high destiny. And this brings us up to the day when he stepped down from his high place to take part in the Christmas pantomime. While she is still thinking thoughts this is a thought she often stumbles on. With a blush she recollects a glimpse of his chest in between when he tore his collar off and when he fell on his knees before the odious Cinderella of that long-gone year. This is not a description of what he did because nobody else remembered him doing it. He tore his collar off. It really happened. And then alas the two uncles playing ugly sisters laughed. This was not of any importance the laughing was in the script. And in the script too she was supposed to step forward with the glass slipper on its cushion. But not in the script was finding herself engrossed in a moment which would last a lifetime. This and a simple slip were not at all the same thing. Oh no simple had nothing to do with it. She found through someone else a way to see herself. She had missed her cue.

I am interested that you mention Lamarck in your letter, but he is too much a genius for me. I need to plod along in my earthy way, counting things and trying to see how they add up. The idea that a mouse might, by sheer force of will, cause its toes to grow long enough for skin to web between and act as wings, that it might IMAGINE becoming a bat—and then become!—this is beyond my scope. The idea charms me, of course it does. But I fight shy of it, because he gives me no proof, and nor do you.

This is all about the cousin at home and the cousin abroad. This is about his letters and her memories. With every letter the letter was in the way. Do you think she tried. No she did not try because it always happened that there was a letter in the way. He wrote about mice imagining they could fly and she remembered how once she had been twenty-two and so unwise as to hang on the brilliant smile of a doctor's son. Not the man with the chest this being one long year after the pantomime was forgotten by everyone else. It was a wastrel if ever there was one. But what had that mattered since he showed himself so astonishingly agile. He can he will he can he said using up everything she thought was hers. Shall I be cherished she asked herself. Already too late. A hopeless episode considering her father would never, no matter how often it is said, never approve. Whereas, Charles.

Charles, her father occasionally introduced the subject of his own accord, though always with the same complaint, young Charles Darwin is a dreamer. Her father said, getting richer. In other ways a steady enough chap, Charles. But a dreamer, her father said.

> These animals interest me very much. Cuvier has arranged them with intestinal worms, though never found within the bodies of other animals. Numerous species inhabit both salt and fresh water; but those to which I allude were found, even in the drier parts of the forest, beneath logs of rotten wood, on which I believe they feed.

There was nothing interesting in her nature that she knew. But here was her cousin writing to her and when he said he will and must and shall she found this tremendously interesting. In a way it was not the most important thing about Charles. The most important thing was that she did not love him. This was the truth. This was the secret and at any rate another matter. And one that was less important than everybody thinks. Everybody thought she did. But to her own astonishment this time it was the other way around. Somebody had to be loved but not her. She said, that is, people said, the people known to her father said, a truth of such kind no young man must ever discover. A truth of such a kind must not be spoken.

Yet she wrote again. Anyhow this is her story.

She wrote again, filling the page with worthy instances. She was a year older. She wrote about the seasickness afflicting him. She had advice. Though she had never been at sea. Do you think not having been at sea would make her say less. Especially for the things he found fascinating. Do any of you know what it is to face the last chance and know it for what it is. Emma had that. So she enthused over his beetles, his worms, his floating islands. Nobody refuses grief.

When someone is away they cannot be spoken to. Even when there are things not to be said. And of course letters are like the very slow and tactical precautions of chess. His next reply started out from the beginning. Think of it. He wrote to her as if he still had all his pieces on the board. Do you begin to see how tactics come into this story. And the letter came bearing still more Chilean postage stamps that proved he was no closer. An entirely different matter is that this meant she could devour everything he had to say with the same scruples as before.

This is such an out of the way place. The goldmine, once reached, is an amazing sight. They say the shaft is a hundred and fifty yards deep. Instead of ladders they prop tree trunks hazardously zig-zagging up the sides with notches cut for footholds.

But to return to the action in the house where Emma's father grew rich and she grew desperate. This is how it was. She had a queer way of thinking. Like thinking down a microscope because she only thought of one thing at a time and it was mostly little things she must put a name to. She turned this queer kind of thought of hers on Charles.

Intuition suggested to her that whereas it was wonderful for him to know such a great deal about the world and nature as he did know, it was more wonderful that he knew so little about women. She accepted this. And then. She described him to herself as an instrument to be played on. He was a harp of nerves. At risk because maybe falling into the hands of some woman, some heartless schemer. The heartless schemer might stand between him and his scientific necessities. There are many women who are not married, though some of them are. Some not. And others would say anything to please.

Labourers carry the rough stone on their backs. Each, loaded with more than his own weight, delivers it to the surface for crushing. I was struck by the pale appearance of the men, many being no more than eighteen or twenty years of age with almost no muscular development. Sweating, they ascend from that great depth up the perilous improvised steps to emerge into the light of the working day. However, I am assured by Mr Nixon, the American who works the mine, that they are not slaves. Their pay, so I am told, is from twenty-six to twenty-eight shillings a month. And they are not allowed to leave the mine more than once in three weeks to spend two days with their families. I know this place must sound harsh to you, but it answers pretty well for the master. And I am not here to judge. I am teaching myself to observe.

Emma would write back. Most certainly she would. And she would write to absolutely say she was shocked. The conditions at the mine shocked her. And his failure to assure her he had felt outrage might only prove Charles was Charles and not that she was herself. But how could he bear to be shown. So she began her letter.

At very least, of this oversight you are guilty, she wrote. My father accuses you of being a dreamer. But I think he is wrong. You are a scientist and one of the best, because you have no fear of looking into things.

However I must protest that I would deplore this neutral passion if it ever came to entail a suspension of the moral imperative.

She found she could be bold in what she told and what remained untold. She had not come from timid people. Or poor people. Though she was shy. And other things passed by. She accepted that. And why. Every day passing by farther and farther out of reach in reality. Nothing changed. Oh dear no. How should a woman's loneliness bother anyone at all. She would write everything. She would write to stop herself thinking.

So think of me at least a little, she wrote, sequestered here in the cool climate of home, obedient to civilised customs, with little to do but watch (right now!) hail dance unheard on the windowsill. My mother has come in and she stands close behind me to read what I am writing. She tut-tuts and asks me to pass on her commiserations. I add to these my prayers for your safe return.

She covered what she next wrote on the silent page. Nothing could be more vulnerable than this. With her free hand she covered it so he would be the only one to read. Think of this naked covering. Nothing could be more exposed. In particular because this was perhaps the only thing he truly hoped to hear.

Ah, but the simple truth, she spelled it out in secret, writing under her hand, is that I envy you the liberty to make your own mistakes.

K n o t s ,   t i e s ,   e t c .

Silence may be a word or, equally, a word missing (missed, most infamously, when it constitutes consent to cruelty). Cymbeline only agrees to speak so that he cannot be said to have yielded by saying nothing. On the other hand a catastrophe might be too far beyond the reach of words. Likewise joy. Plus, come to think of it, there is a kind of active headache, as many among us know, adept at braiding sounds together in the mute chamber of the brain and twisting them into a knot tight enough to hobble the capacity for thinking straight at all.

Commander J. Irving's 1884 revision of *Knots, Ties and Splices* by J. Tom Burgess (published London:

Routledge & Kegan Paul Ltd) steps aside from informing mariners of the day and—through later reprints—truck drivers and others, who might need to secure haulage loads or fellow mountaineers, to offer just one item of advice which implies social, perhaps even political, application.

'In its double shape the running loop, under the name the Tomfool Knot (Fig. 20) has achieved greater renown than almost any other knot of modern times. It is made in the beginning like the running knot (Fig. 21), after which the firm end is passed through the open simple knot so as to form a double loop or bow.' He proceeds to explain that if a person's hands or wrists are placed through the open loops C and D, and the latter are then drawn tight and the loose ends tied firmly round the centre, a pair of improvised handcuffs may be made, from which it will need more than ordinary skill or strength to escape. 'The firmness and security of such a knot depends, however, upon the rope used being well stretched; otherwise a person with small hands would not have much difficulty in releasing himself from this or any other knot made in a rope.'

Typical, that a book entirely concerned with the practicalities of knot-tying does not once address the symbolic implications of such knots: neither the knot as a hindrance to a woman's pregnancy (as the Cotton Vitall MS, *Cockayne* Leechdom I [c.1050] has it: the evil has been done to a man [by a knot] so that he may not enjoy his lusts)—nor the knot as a Christian protection against evil (patently unsuccessful for much of the Middle Ages)—nor the knot as a cure for warts (as still practised in some dogged corners of Britain)—nor even the Buddhist knot (one of the Eight Auspicious Signs)—let alone that symbol of eternity and much else besides, the Mystic Knot of Vishnu.

The heart of the matter is that when we undo a knot we are metaphorically reaching the centre, the cabalistic unravelling of thought. Neither Commander Irving nor Mr Burgess, as the case may be, is concerned to tell us anything more than how to *tie* knots. On the subject of how to untie them they have nothing to say.[1]

Come to think of it, there is a kind of active headache adept at braiding sounds together in the mute chamber of the brain, as many among us know, and twisting them into a knot tight enough to hobble the least capacity for thinking straight at all. On the other hand joy might be too far beyond the reach of words. Likewise catastrophe. Cymbeline only agrees to speak so that he cannot be said to have yielded by saying nothing. Silence may be a word missing (missed, most infamously, when it constitutes consent to cruelty) or, equally, just a word.

---

[1] May have ironic application to the book you hold in your hand right now.

T V reporter

We are walking among the dried eaten-out turds of a
village not in our own country of course——saying at
least our television viewers (good evening) are safe
from the stench but still agreeing that if you were to
be shut up and suffocating for air you'd breathe this
gratefully and with relief

We are photographing the children with distorting
cameras that bloat them into abstract works of art——
I feel my eyeballs (fingers swollen with regrets) it
takes the power of will to look

Would these be pigs' turds?—and something incredible
there are holes in the ground where things have lived
or live—we (walking the baked dust these foreign
people venerate) are the very objects we've been
trying to recognize

Children watch us silently—there is no word for us

N o i s e

My dear cousin,

I see no way out, I must withhold nothing of the whole tale so far as it is known to me. Even now I am still on my mission to clear up the last details to be yielded by the colony. Having brought to the task my knowledge of our Uncle John, as we have known him since we were boys, your father's kindness to him and, in turn, your own kindness, the protected life that your family still provides and mine supports. I cannot think you have any idea of the case I am unearthing—other than that, when we used to frighten each other with guesses at the dark secret in his life, we did not imagine a fraction of it. Such hopes as I brought with me that despite his ruined state he might emerge as a pattern of truth, sincerity and decency were deeply, deeply misguided.

I do not quite know how to write what I need to say next, but I trust you will acknowledge the cost of saying it: I cannot ignore what I have learned, I cannot lay up yet more horrors of the conscience in remaining silent, yet neither do I dare speak of it to any but you. We were very young to hope for something good. Do not be angry with me for saying so. In spirit, in moral decency, as in the conduct of his business, is every man not obliged to be solvent? The decision of what *you* do is essentially yours, he lives with you. I have reason to know, by this time, that there is no good in him and no prospect *for* him. Too much evil is in this. Even now I have not a clear idea how deep it goes. I have not the power of counting such things.

Setting out, I began with what we already knew— his life with us in Gloucestershire—safe and settled, dedicated to surround himself with that constant din which is so maddening to all, driven as he is (no one knew whence or how) by what we have humoured as his eccentricity. His eternal kettle sizzling on the hob, his birds twittering in uncovered cages, his clocks set to different times so they chime continually, erratically and infuriatingly throughout every hour in that corner of your idyllic home I now recognize as hell, the windmill's offset vanes clattering at the least breeze, wires strung among the trees to whine the whole while, even the creek roaring through his mill race ... each piece a part of the puzzle. Imagine the sheer energy needed to equip your garden with all those contraptions we used to think incompetently made because they screeched and knocked. They are as he meant them to be: strident enough to drown out the terrible silence in his mind.

This is my conclusion. I have begun to understand that he fears the slightest hiccup in the fabric of sound. A mere blip of nothing might be enough to drop him back into the abyss of what he has done.

It troubled me even as a child, and it troubles me now, more nearly, to witness his loneliness (having what I have to tell) and think what he did to bring it about. You say you are happy to pursue your chosen way of indulgence, even at the cost of the anxiety he occasions in you. But I must warn you of the reason behind these eccentricities, his madness as I now prefer to call it, which you have a right to know. The cold and irrevocable Nemesis, the blight ruining everything it rests on, is Guilt. He did *not* return home from the colonies of his own free will. He escaped. Stage by stage, imagine: using a false name he bribes his way aboard ship and then works his passage. At the first foreign port he finds work as an overseer on a rubber plantation where natives milk the trees for a Malacca-based company, but it seems that even the lowliest labourers soon sense a secret crime and speak of him as The Man with a Hole for a Head. I have it firsthand. He vanishes for a year until he arrives on your father's doorstep and is welcomed in.

That's when he knew he had got away with it.

Society, which has taken upon itself the general arrangement of the whole system of filling its coffers at the cost of human freedom for others (whether convicts or slaves) did *not* deliver the expected returns for our Uncle John. It did not enrich him as promised. So he, with misdirected energy, came to seize what he thought of as his due. You may imagine how grieved I am to write these words. It went wrong. Hence he escaped, hence he must hide from his guilt at the bottom of your garden and build around him a shield (incidentally) of the comforts of clean linen, cups of tea and almshouse duties, having reassumed his family name and been welcomed with kindness by your family and mine, also (essentially) that shield of noise. Oh, how the threat of quiet must besiege him with deadly persistence. Our parents had the delicacy to accept that, for whatever reason, he was a man in hiding within himself. Many's the time I've eavesdropped on whispered family conferences. Fearful lest the least probe into the *what* or *when* of his condition might trigger a fit of madness in him, the snarls and screeches of some horrid tale of colonial isolation and hardship, they behaved as if nothing was amiss, at least so far as to write each Christmas to his parents back in New South Wales assuring them he was safe and well. And what did those parents—their sister and brother-in-law—write back? Nothing. That is to say, a great deal of inconsequential prattle: but *nothing* of the truth, the whole of which they undoubtedly knew. I should like to have questioned them while here, such is my anger, though of course both are now dead. Meanwhile your father took him in and humoured him with superfluous duties till he grew middle aged, stately, fat and popular with children—especially us boisterous ones.

But what must he have been going through ever since he sold himself to the Enemy? What must he still?

Like as he is to be seen nightly, staring into the moon's blind eye, what he hears is what no other mortal can hear: the startled cries of Aboriginal women, himself reining in his horse while he turns in the saddle to face the men he leads, men who have agreed 'to teach these savages a lesson they will not forget' and who still remember him as a spirited lad. One of them rallied to bring the sight alive for me, saying he 'wore his triumph like I don't know what, sir, a crown'. Well, cousin, those 'savages' had turned out to be a harmless few, twenty-eight people in all, taking refuge from the heat of the day, found seated in the shade around their little cooking fires. What he lives with is knowing that, even so, he spurred his horse and urged the fellows with cutlasses to follow. Nightmare upon nightmare he must hear again the whisk of his service sword, blood as I was told 'guttering' from an old man's throat, a heartbroken female tenderly murmuring to a bloodied child 'for all the world like a mother'. That's the account of it as witnessed by two who were there. His fellows, convict labourers assigned to neighbouring properties, hacked away at their work (among them a black African from Liverpool), their horses 'stumbling among sticky stones'. Some must have leapt down because their 'daggers flashed in the sunlight'. The victims shrieked until there was no more shrieking and the only sound was the sizzle as 'chunks of the corpses, hands and heads chopped off, were thrown on the flames'. How those shrieks must burrow and go on burrowing into his brain!

Be it what it may have seemed at the time, this chopping and burning of the bodies constituted proof, of course, and a form of confession, as you must see for yourself. Regardless of how ignorant he probably was when setting out at the head of his party, by *then* Uncle John knew he had committed a crime. A court case ensued, which proved anything but straightforward. Indeed the issue went to trial twice, thanks to the perseverence of the governor, Sir Geo. Gipps, and these details have been witnessed. He (Uncle John) trusted to fire to obliterate all trace of his victims, identity impossible to reconstruct from charred lumps and smashed bones of assorted sizes, the evidence reduced to a stench, airborne and swirling away as greasy smoke ... all gone by the time the Sydney investigator arrived at the scene.

His men, nonetheless, were charged and bound over and the governor saw to it that seven were hanged. It was so famous a case it brought the colony to the brink of revolution because the killing of natives would henceforth be punishable as murder. But our Uncle John was nowhere to be found nor apprehended, leaving his illiterate fellows to bear the blame. Thus began his unthinkable flight—a gentleman wanted by the law—

riding off alone with his mother's prayer that he might survive to seek refuge in a neighbour's cupboard or under stairs, and each at a different house, in hay sheds and lofts and—who knows?—under beds, then to the best of my belief in a boat paddling down the Gwydir River and sleeping out, a gift of gold sovereigns hidden in his socks, till he reached the fringes of Sydney town. Such is the haunted picture he presents, desperate, grubby and unshaven, an iron barrier between him and decent society, which nothing now could remove. Scouring the quay for a skipper disreputable enough to sign him on (no pay, in return for no questions asked, so it seems), he found one. Even as his ship cleared the Heads, how can it be otherwise than that he knew it was futile to congratulate himself that his mother's prayers had been answered: God could not now possibly exist.

Such was his life as an escapee back in 1838 when he was young and without the least remorse.

And we came to know him as a moody dog, at home yet not at home, shut away inside himself, crowded in by that infernal racket of his own making. Inevitably, for dreadful moments at a time, rends must happen in the web of sound he has created for protection and then no doubt his memories of Myall Creek leap to life. Yes, heart crying out at the pain, for he has a heart or he would not be in hiding. Doubtless the silence reminds him, too, of those companions hanged—the first Englishmen to be condemned by English law for such murders—and those spared the hangman led away in chains, even while he, John Fleming, the only freeborn murderer among them, protected by settlers of his own class, and the one to get off, got out. Young still at the time. Free still. Think of it! Free!

It is the fearful peculiarity of his condition that, at any hour of his life, he must anticipate discovery, and at any opening of the door or pull of the bell at your garden gate, or any delivery of a letter (such as this) aware that his secret may take air and fire and explode in his face. Such is his life of safety!

As soon as I am able I shall bring the documents so far to hand, though there is nothing to be got from them but sorrow. Then, you should be warned, I shall pass the whole matter over to you. I most earnestly entreat and beg you to decide, by that juncture, what shall be done.

Till my return, your faithful cousin,

Rupert.

Li River

Broad and tranquil, the Li River meanders among a cluster of mountains jutting up from the plain. Wisps of early fog having briefly veiled river and rice paddies rise, fray and evaporate to disclose pinnacles so spectacular one might be excused for objecting that such exaggerated shapes belong only in ink-and-brush drawings by Chinese masters of a bygone age. Yet here is where the hired motor barge unarguably glides through the hazy sunshine of a new day, its wake gently belatedly breaking as scrolls of old gold along either bank at the rim of a landscape perpetually closing in—as witnessed by our film crew gathered on deck—hundreds upon hundreds of rocky crags crowding to the banks so that, at each bend ahead, the bright banner of water unfurls to open out an ever-kaleidoscoping vista of cliffs crowned with vegetation. Copses of motionless trees, buds breaking open, the mountains growing taller as they are looked at, air a weir of light and the clouds like great white rocks sailing above the drift of the current as it moves through their dark shadows. Momentarily there seems not enough air to breathe. Then suddenly canyons rupture and the stone clouds roll apart for a storm of light to break loose over everything. Nor do the mountains just stand where they are: they move, too, each on its own majestic turntable.

The awestruck cast (and even a few jaded stars) point out lonely shrines, picturesque hovels. Half-submerged water buffalo, snorting as they bask in the cool, wallow under sheets of silk among the inverted peaks. Then, on its leisurely progress toward the sea and in the certainty of brightness, the river unrolls the ancient city of Guilin for our inspection, only to let it pass, unstopped at.

Without doubt this film, a period piece featuring missionary nuns, a courageous doctor and his alienated wife, is going to have to measure up to distractingly gorgeous visuals. The location the scout negotiates has the whole crew buzzing: a timber house overlooking an expanse of water that curves to the right around a tongue of flat land raked with lines of rice and outlined by a deeply shadowed band of forest beyond. The finishing touch is a paid fisherman already in position down there, seated in his skiff, tame cormorant perched on the prow—a throttle round its throat to prevent swallowing what it catches—all mirrored by the stillness.

The first shoot is soon set up. The director, choosing to begin with a simple wordless episode from late in the story, explains that to have this in the can will set the tone for everything else. It's a scene where the heroine experiences an epiphany: in a flash of inspiration she knows she must put the past behind her and accept that, as yet, there is no future. She must live in the present … the terrifying present of a cholera epidemic. Last-minute adjustments are made to the original 1920s frock she wears. And the make-up people improve details of flushed cheeks and perspiration appropriate for a hotter day than nature provides.

'She walks across the verandah. So, at the rail,' the director explains to our new young star and she nods a trifle nervously, making her own final check of the skirt with its tasselled sash, 'at the rail she gazes down on the river. She gazes down on the reflected mountains—no, try it with your body half-turned that way—yes, lovely—perfect. She knows about the fatal disease emptying the fields of labourers, a tragedy—yes, good—she can see dead bodies stretched out at the water's edge—good, yes, though she's perhaps more troubled by the sight, do you think?—horror—hands, yes, because a sense of foreboding—desperately afraid, afraid, afraid of the plague, afraid the frightened peasants might soon resort to violence—they are superstitious—blaming foreigners like her for the agony their families are suffering—she faces the fact that she may have only these few minutes of safety left, up here above the village—perfect. And again—just like that. Roll cameras. Action.'

'What the fuck!' shouts a nearby voice and an echo of similar protests ripples through the crew distributed about the location.

The director himself stares at his monitor screen in disbelief. Slap bang in centre frame, impertinently upright on the dirt track traversing our empty rice field on the other side of the river, just where his young star's gaze is directed, two men have appeared from nowhere. Chinese. Some sort of locals. Our plague-emptied middle distance ruined.

'Where did those guys come from?' people ask and spread empty hands to demonstrate innocence of blame. Already runners are on their way down the slope, waving and calling out across the water. They signal wildly and bellow through megaphones. But no amount of fuss seems to attract the attention of the intruders, an old man and a young man, who continue strolling together, deep in conversation. The old one, dressed in baggy peasant pants, loose shirt and conical wicker hat pauses; so the young one, a workman perhaps, in jeans and t-shirt much like anybody, must also pause. All available members of the film crew, jumping about like rabbits, now try to attract the attention of the fisherman, mid-stream in a skiff with his dreaming bird, for him to pass the message on. But he has been paid good money on condition he takes no notice of anything, however weird. Whatever may happen, we ourselves told him, he and his cormorant must fish all day regardless. Dedicated to the task in hand, he turns out to be a man of his word. He hears but does not hear our interpreter beg him to row over to the other side and pass word to the trespassers at present ruining the shot.

★

Master and disciple, having observed a commotion on the far bank of the river and noted with surprise the absence of passing tourist boats, stand contemplating the scene in all its splendour. The remote babble of the foreigners, *waiguoren*, with big cameras on cranes and vehicles parked at odd angles is amusing in its way. Side by side they move in stillness, knowing each other so well. Their destiny has led them here to the white radiance of understanding, which is where they must part. Time suspended. The young one frames a question in mind. The question takes the shape of years of patient study, a question which, even as he asks, is heard—though never actually spoken.

Disciple's thought: So finally, master, as we go our different ways, what *is* the Dao?

Master's thought: This is the secret of secrets. I can only tell you if you have conquered your enslavement to the illusions of the temporal world.

Disciple's thought: I have already conquered my enslavement to the illusions of the temporal world.

Master's thought: And because the Dao is indeed the secret of secrets I can only tell you when you have mastered all the words in all the languages of the world.

They stand in that old gold hazy stillness of knowing. The remote gesticulation of the film crew ceases to exist. The fisherman, his cormorant and skiff (and the reflection of the fisherman with his cormorant and skiff) cease to exist.

Disciple's thought: I have mastered all the words in all the languages of the world. I am ready to hear.

Master's thought: Then I have already told you.

Book burial

The East is dark. Far beneath the cruising aircraft lies a sleeping land that mirrors the stars. The dark land a web of sparkling lights. Seen from above it shows itself as the stilled slice of everything. No one can say what it isn't. But what it is is a time-form, complete in all respects, this eternal *now.* For the illuminated roads connect a lacework of empty towns even beyond the curve of earth. The East is dark. The relentless clock changes its evidence: 2:45 am. Another timeframe: 2:46 am. Another: 2:47 am. Each complete and never to occur again.

Down on the ground it is simply night. Dull ordinary night. Dust puffs up higher than the houses. Up into the dark. Gasoline fumes clog the invisible air. On the ground it is not at all like a mirror of the stars. It is dark and choked with the foul-smelling dust. For those awake, the night is simply night. Though some awake have work to do. Big trucks give off the fumes and kick up the dust. Their headlamps cluster here and there around appointed garbage dumps, around abandoned gullies and handy bomb craters left over from that old war so disastrously lost. Headlamps cluster where men work through the night in the dust, busy round a hundred pits, craters and dumps all across the landscape. Huge holes already half full of books. Which is why there are arc lamps too. The lamps glare down into the gaping earth. Also why bulldozers wait at night's rim. Each with a driver whose orders are to stand by till the last truck backs out and then move in to complete the earthmoving. That's what he has been told. There is plenty to do, with millions more books on their way. Soon to be delivered. Who ever thought there could be so many? Most of them, when you get a good look, new. A slagheap of books with glossy covers. Books scheduled to be buried in the vast grave of garbage dumps. Each minute ticking over is some writer's last. And sure enough long lines of heavy vehicles arrive full and depart empty. The East is dark. Gasoline fumes clog the air. Waiting holes yawn up at the night sky. Each hole the centre of converging headlamps. High overhead an aircraft roars away in the distance. It has a long way to go. The country is big.

And there is one, an old man of twenty. He is so thin and so pale and so blue, leaning on the rake he has been issued. Grasping the rake with moon-pale hands. He asks: 'Is this us? Are we doing this?' Another man with the same brand of rake does not reply, looking at him as if he's crazy. And the world turns for the next minute to pass. 'Get on with it,' he growls at last, 'we've got this job here, haven't we?' And they use their rakes to scrape up any books that land on the rim and push them in. 'But, I mean,' says the old man of twenty, 'is this what we must do from now on?' His arms are thin. Deep shadows haunt his eyes. 'The wall is a thing of the past,' the other says, 'that should be enough. And me and you ... we're getting paid to work.' They rake some more. Little clouds of breath escaping into the long November night. The old-young man, so pale and blue, admits, 'I suppose it's one big party!'

The East is dark. An aircraft cruises high above a web of sparkling lights. The sleeping land a peaceful mirror of the stars. Empty towns and roads lie on the land as lacework. Everything down there is *now*. Nowhere left out. The clock stealthily changes evidence: 3:51 am. Another timeframe: 3:53 am. At an army base away in the west the ferment of urgency is alive with officers consulting maps. A task to be done. A plan to coordinate. The supervision of a thousand commandeered trucks— the entire military fleet plus every available small-time van and empty semi-trailer—to be driven across the border through the dead of night. Secrecy essential. A newly liberated populace to be freed from doubt. By order. The atmosphere is cheerful.

Down on the ground it is simply night. Each truck, a link in the grand design, connecting two fixed points: a bookshop, a dump. Radio contact crackles repeated warnings of the deadline. Police coordinate to keep the roadways clear. The scale absolute. The sense of holiday infectious. In all directions for a hundred thousand square kilometres the intersections are kept clear. The operation proceeds. To bury an idea, nothing less tremendous than that. A bloodless coup. Secrecy essential for success. Every book on sale to be struck down before the new day dawns, cleared from mind, irretrievable as passing time and altogether buried under cover of night. Every last one taken out. The cleansing absolute with no exceptions. For nothing escapes history. The eradication of history itself being history. And the death of an idea implicit in the idea. The greatness of an idea its doom.

All Europe sleeps. Except booksellers living above their premises, who hear the lock burst and the downstairs door being smashed, who stand at the top of the stairs still in their dressing-gowns, speechless, shocked and helpless while workmen swarm in among the shelves—some with uniforms and insignia, others local garbage guys. Neighbours on either side lie low in bed, with no idea what's going on, thanking their lucky stars that they are not the ones in trouble. They do not have a bookshop. But here the frightened owners in their night clothes stand at the top of the stairs and watch intruders armed with axes and crowbars trundling skips, pushing makeshift trolleys and wheelbarrows and tipping the stock off the shelves. Clearing out every book that can be found. No time for exceptions. Carting the books off to a truck in the street. With them goes the breathable air. Leaving only dust. Dust, wrecked shelves and homeless communities of silverfish. Then the trespassers tramp back to nail up the smashed door in case there may be money on the premises, furnishings—temptations of whatever sort. Looting and theft by amateurs on no account condoned. Through the letterbox they post an open letter promising an Owners' Compensation Package to include fresh basic stock (approved titles) but not before the purpose is accomplished and the idea buried.

The truck waits at the door. Motor idling. At last the driver can get going. He clashes his gears and rumbles away along the long long road, the long lonely road of witnessing streetlamps, toward the designated crater or the tip with its bulldozer parked beside a ready heap of soil. The driver on his radio reports position and progress. Police cars are at the intersections of the long and empty road. Lights lights lights passing, their square reflections peeling off his windscreen as he drives. Books heaped in the back joggle soundlessly. In the dark. Soundless along the empty road and around the empty turnings. Books joggle right behind the driver who drives them through the empty night. To their destruction. And now he meets another truck. There are two trucks on the long long road. Three. And now a van. Ahead he sees the arc lights of the garbage dump. Cheerful police wave him through. Not a hitch. Smooth as surgery the books arrive. This is how it is. Dust puffs up at the dump. Foul-smelling dust. He swings his vehicle to join the glare of headlights shafting through the dust-smothered night, greeted by the thunder of revving bulldozers.

The old man of twenty, blue and thin with moon-pale hands, rakes at any books that land on the rim, pushing the last few into the hole. 'What about them who give the orders?' he says. 'Do they know why we're doing this?' The other growls, 'Of course they do. The guys with power know.' He rakes some more to safely bury them. 'But do they?' asks the one with a rake in his moon-pale hands because it's hard even to believe in his own life having a reason. And, if he were more used to voicing doubts he might well add, 'What if this is all for nothing?' But he does not have the habit. And nor does he have a reason really. Just that books don't seem to him the right thing for bulldozers to bury.

Instead he surprises himself with two completely different thoughts. One thought he speaks out loud. 'Of course, this is what we've all been praying for.' The other thought he keeps to himself. And he looks round him at the dust-choked night, at the dump where he works, in case somewhere in the wreckage he himself might catch a glimpse of certainty, just a glimpse. 'There's something wrong,' he nearly says out loud but thinks the better of it just in time. All with no idea where these books are coming from or why they must be buried. Nothing of bookshops gutted of books and boarded up. Nor that an officer at army headquarters repeats the order that this fact must not, repeat not, be reported in the press. That is the point.

Let the country sleep undisturbed and wake to just another day of joyful reunions. Forget the fact that all across the sleeping land are bookshops with shattered doors and gaping shelves, bookshops boarded up by the very men who broke them down. The men who post an open letter through the smashed letterbox. The freight of dust boarded up. Hammers poised in the frozen moment of 4:08 am. The job done. 4:11 am. Pits and dumps filled before daybreak. Everyone paid overtime.

The East is dark. Seen from above and numerous as stars, sparkling lights converge on craters in the ground. Nothing will serve but burial. Burning, though that tradition goes way back, is known to take too long. And people are persistent when it comes to harbouring their prejudices ... otherwise known as hopes. Lights mirror the stars. Liberation from doubt to be delivered on the doorstep by morning. Welcome to the Free World.

A D   1 0 0 0

Day like a great rock. The first day in the Year of Our
Lord 1000. Thus a man Adam by name and known
as the Ready. Son of a law-speaker, though himself a
peasant. Simple in garb, stands Godly on watch. He
stands on watch awaiting the dawn, Adam the Ready
in the last of the dark, his old axe Ironflank bright aloft,
wife Gudrun at his side. The sodden swamp of winter
lies on the land around. Themselves braced ready for
the first day which shall be the last. The rime-cold
marsh grass flat, a rattling raspberry stands against the
wind with sticks a-clatter. Ghosts sigh through sedge.
They wait without let, this Adam and Gudrun. They

alone dare gaze at the dark tower dark at world's edge. Left by Romans who crucified Our Lord. The tower of slaughterers' stones locked in place and built with the Devil's cunning. They gaze at that tower and the ruined gate beside. The river between as slow as melted lead. Without let they wait. The good man Adam and Gudrun his wife. Wait for the day of the Holy Grail, the cup that held the blood of Christ. Wait for the sun to show his face and God to appear in wrath and mercy. The last of all the world's days breaks. A glim of sky tints the clouds and the axe aloft. A glim on the ground creeps to the tombstones underfoot. Creeps to frost-hard tussocks and ghosts among the sedge and rattling canes. Sure enough the ground begins to crawl about. Wife and man watch graveyard slabs by their own will shift. Long shadows crawl on the mud where bloodless fingers gripple the lip of open graves. And mossy heads with slime-clogged locks and rotted swaddlings lift their fleshless limbs and faces. Children among the olders, whom time and plague have eaten out, turn like flowers to greet the eternal light. The virtuous, hasty with their greed for praise, arise. They rise to hear the Last Trumpet blast in glory. Rise to claim their seat at God's right hand. Thus watched at dawn by Adam who was first and now is last and Adam's good wife. The ghastly dead stand tall to claim eternal life. Stand the difficult standing at resurrection's dreadful pull.

But the blare of angel trumpets never sounds. The witnesses see nothing but the sun. The sun glides up unheralded. Light lips the rim of yet another ordinary day of toil.

Winners

I know them ... you see, I know these people ... the
ones who stand for law and order ... law and order!
made out of nothing ... clearing the decks for healthy
greed, that's what ... clearing the decks alright, so get
this through your head ... they sit on their fat backsides
in offices and call it work ... some nerve! ... and more
and more there are desperate people haunting our streets
like that man slouched over his cardboard sign on which
he has printed HOMELESS HUNGRY HELP ... he
expects compassion ... hell, no! ... wrong city, wrong
country ... this place is wealthy and spending up big
... not for the likes of him to spoil people's fun with his

complaints or his squashed cap on the footpath between his knees ... what does he think! ... the very idea that we are honest-to-God social, responsible, civilised citizens takes the cake! ... no way, not since the death of society when Margaret Thatcher led the world in a triumphal rampage back to some sort of Dark Ages of the striving individual ... each for himself or herself ... and don't forget how we leapt on the idea, too ... it also took *us* to make it true ... Thatcher alone was nothing but a ranting politician ... the homeless, indeed! ... so, a few passing people throw away their loose change? ... the pirates of the stock exchange will have something to say about this over morning coffee in the city, but for now they can't stop, they can't be stopped ... they're in a hurry to get to a business lunch ... a punishing schedule when you come to think ... the homeless are no subject for consideration among those who work for their living and live by standards and stand on their own two feet ... you know what I'm saying? ... with money in the bank ... Amen ... nor is homelessness a subject for the homeless, because when you don't have a place to live it's so much *the* subject that you'll talk about anything but ... and your life's so busy too ... so planned ... you know, planned around places of possible refuge, comfort, lavatories public and otherwise ... opening hours and closing hours, warm spots for shelter, places to wash and sit ... food ... how far you need to walk ... how safe to jump the tram ... bakeries known to give away yesterday's stale stock if you get there in time, police evasion, oh all manner of necessities ... better to talk to the homeless about epistemology or suicide, Substance & Illusion and the New Science of Giambattista Vico ... take a guy like this with his head in his hands, cradling the weight of his brain and mystified by it, he'd understand the saints ... though maybe not the point of becoming one if you've had your throat cut or been crucified upside down ... and no doubt he knows better than most how to debate with a Trappist who's not allowed to hold up his end of a pleasant altercation ... so he comes down to this, perhaps because he's the culprit of something ... hunched over a cardboard homeless sign ... life going from bad to worse ... quite young with greasy hair to hide his face ... saying nothing, quite mum ... trusting the written word to speak for him ... because, in the telling, he mightn't quite get it clear ... well, for starters, he might break down ... maybe you'll object that he's doing what he can ... because admittedly it isn't easy to put oneself out there on the street ... but this is not a thing the winners can ever be expected to appreciate ... no point asking passers by who *do* pass by how they would feel

if ... hmm, hmm ... you see my point? ... get real! ...
HOMELESS HUNGRY HELP ... homeless, indeed!
he's lucky they don't kick him in the face for spoiling
the serenity of their day ... he's lucky they don't yank his
old jacket off him, split his chest and rip out his guts, the
pearly ball of his intestines, heart spouting startled blood,
rightness is on their side because loudness is rightness ...
word is that they've never been otherwise ... and I might
as well tell you this is not exactly news ... they were
the same when I was a kid ... they had no less cause to
smile back then ... they are the same as they were when
the war broke out ... and when the next war broke out
and all the wars since ... they are the same as they were
when they fought to keep segregation and apartheid
and laws against the poor doing what the rich took for
granted ... don't imagine this will change just because
of the brilliant Julian Assanges of the world who insist
on popping up now and then ... way back they were
the ones burning witches and smashing works of art and
they'll happily do it again ... they were the ones to cram
Indentured Labour on board the slave ships out of Africa,
to cram the streets of Nuremberg in adoring multitudes
sometime later ... tarara-boomdee-ay! ... pocketing
profits when the stock exchange tumbled ... always the
same crew ... hypocrites, bullshit artists, genteel thugs

... they're still up for plundering villages and raping the helpless, they'll torture anyone for having unfamiliar ideas ... all the more readily if there's oil to be had or precious minerals the locals have no use for ... even the passive ones among them are catered for, sitting with equanimity in suburban livingrooms to watch asylum seekers drown in leaky boats on television ... they come from a long line that goes way back ... they were a bad start for any country and they're going to be an even worse finish ... but don't imagine for a moment they are without secrets ... ssh ssh ... they have secrets right enough ... like every tinpot tyrant and tyrantess, every bureaucrat, every hope-smasher and heretic-murderer in history ... and the biggest of those secrets is ignorance ... at all costs they will protect this precious ignorance of theirs to pass down to their brats like a congenital disease ... they *don't* know and they don't *want* to know ... despite, now and again, a suffocating shadow getting stuck in the windpipe and choking them by surprise ... though in general they survive these little interruptions and reminders of mortality to do another deal, fix another contract, outwit another rival ... whatever ... it's all so sporting, matey, casual, so horribly Australian ... you can't mean this one wearing an Ermenegildo Zegna suit? ... I surely do! ... compassion's an odd quirk

his kind doesn't have the stomach for, a lethal drug ...
well, because it dulls judgement, scores no goals and pays
no dividend ... they don't have the temperament for it
either, it's a constitutional thing, a medical condition and
nobody to blame ... what they do have is the rage to
purge, to clear things out and knock stuff down ... it's a
world of quick responses, theirs ... hit the button before
you think ... on sale everywhere ... if the Americans
do, then what else is there to say? ... don't just take my
word for it ... they'll swear blind that the market is God,
don't you know by now? ... HOMELESS HUNGRY
HELP ... plagiarism anyway! ... they keep going and
that's how you can tell who they are ... they don't waste
their breath ... they say nothing because there's nothing
to be said ... and if you drive on drugs you are out of
your mind, okay?

Glider pilot

Both craft safely airborne, the biplane glimmers fish-like ahead of him as it dips sharply, allowing the tow rope enough slack to slip free, and then banks up and away across the evening sky. Enclosed in his cockpit he always registers this moment of liberty because his glider sighs, easing its slender ribs, righting the long spine from the tip of its greyhound nose to the tuck of its tail. No longer stressed with the drag of external power. Tilting by discriminating degrees into the wind.

The last shaft of sunlight glances off the dwindling biplane ahead (that's good old Tony out there) to stamp the aircraft, like a silver cross of Lorraine, aslant on the emptiness. The earth below is already veiled in night, the earth of home. He scans his map board, consults his compass and checks the instrument panel. Satisfied with his climbing altitude and the course set, the pilot lifts the goggles strapped to his leather helmet and fits them down over his face.

Gradually, gradually the remaining light evaporates from the sky—whisked aside, ahead of him, just like that—and he has the sensation of dropping into darkness, although from experience he knows better than to doubt the altimeter glowing phosphorescently among other indicators of survival. The precision structure which encases him sings its subtle, deep vibration. All is well. He lets out a long-held breath. So far so good.

A swift low-lying cloud feathers against his windscreen to drift behind and he thinks about the theory that, supposing outer space were ever reached, incredible speeds would induce a sensation of such stillness loose objects could float, weightless, about one's head. A sheen of moonlight far below glazes the hammered-metal sea. In half an hour, he knows, the coast of France will creep across, corroding this lovely brightness, eating it away till nothing but a total void is left. And does. France, the defeated land. He feels a remote thunder of shame loom beneath him like a whale. The secret claustrophobia of air-raid sirens seeming already to worm deep into the inner ear. Cymbals of stored light clashing twice only as he blinks.

Entombed, he has nothing now to sustain his faith but the interpretation of a grid and the mathematical tables he has learned by heart. Pure geometry. Triangulating infinity. He discovers what it is to inhabit a pyramid, passively to watch the last stone—in the last doorway to the only passage connecting his chamber to the light—set in place.

Dials glow dimly and he ponders the mystery of phosphorus, of plankton at sea, waves folding on a seashore, fleeting traces of light among sand granules, of cause and effect, of the philosophy of being. And like flecks of this same phosphorus, momentary glitters spangle the void below. Tiny imperfections in the blackout blanketing every other sign of civilisation, a betrayal of towns expecting bombs, towns which must certainly be ringed by batteries of anti-aircraft guns.

Occupied territory.

A gentle cough from somewhere behind him interrupts his reverie. A man's cough. The hair bristles on the back of his neck. Then comes a furtive rustle of thick clothing. But he knows, of course he does, he remembers: there are six men packed in the hollow belly of his glider.

Didn't they shake hands with him, one by one, out of respect for death? Blood-warm hands? Each man with a parachute strapped to his back? Having flown them beyond the notion of a frontline already, he must now reach the right coordinates for them to jump. He cannot fail them. He must not. Their destination known to him alone.

The paratrooper squad sits, patient with the admirable patience of trained men. At his word, as he is aware, they are ready to cast themselves out into the dark sky with the inexplicable abandon of courage. Fighters. Each one hunched round his secrets of love and fear, each one unmistakable as anybody else, each one a stranger. This is the mission. They know what they know must be done. As he knows what he knows. No need to speak. And, once free of his human cargo, he will steer the silent glider to sweep across the thermals, razoring wings righting as he turns for home ... doubtless in the stab of searchlights and between the first bursts of shellfire.

But, just now, war is this and only this: a state of suspension in the unheard power of knowing.

Notes

A contributing factor to the silences being explored is that most of these pieces engage with a 'silent' partner, being written as if by others: by the anonymous Anglo-Saxon poet of *The Wanderer*, by King Alfred the Great, Sir Joseph Banks, Charles Dickens, Henry James, Joseph Furphy, Gerard Manley Hopkins, Gertrude Stein, James Joyce, Hermann Broch, Louis-Ferdinand Céline, Bruno Schulz, William Faulkner, Henry Green, Samuel Beckett, Malcolm Lowry, Wolfgang Borchert and Gabriel García Márquez.

Of course, these tributes do not pretend to be more than echoes, intonations and the structures of reason—the actual voices of the originals will always embody an underlying subconscious energy unique to the writer and impossible to reproduce, since voice is indissolubly bound up with what we have to say.

Some are freely based on fact (such as the presentation of Captain Cook's thigh to his crew), others are entirely factual (as with the threatening fax sent anonymously to Judith Wright), but most are fiction. In certain cases references are built into the text (as with Abraham Lincoln's Gettysburg address), making a separate note redundant. Specific voices and references which may not be self-evident are as follows:

'Semaphore': Wolfgang Borchert, *The Man Outside.*

'The Rigatti Motet': developed from John Milton's mention of catching a distant, myopic glimpse of this enthronement in 1638, in *Defensio Secunda*. While in Florence Milton met many poets and intellectuals, including Galileo—then old and blind and still officially a prisoner of the Inquisition. Milton's contemporary, Giovanni Rigatti (b. Venice, 1615) was already famous as a composer, appointed *maestro di cappella* at Udine Cathedral when he was just twenty.

'Hartmund Eischlbeck': James Joyce. The quotation embedded here is from *Ulysses.*

'James Cook': Sir Joseph Banks, *Journal*.

'A Conservationist': Bruno Schulz, *Sanatorium Under the Sign of the Hourglass*. The poem quoted is 'Silence' by Judith Wright. I was present at the same afternoon tea with Mr Giri, the president of India, in 1970, when, to his amusement, her deafness led to several abrupt changes of subject. Many years later, at Judith Wright's house, she showed me the fax quoted here.

'Talkad': Gerard Manley Hopkins, *Notebook*. This temple is still buried under the dunes.

'L'Étoile Bleue': autobiographical incident, 1959.

'A toast': Henry Green, *Concluding*.

'The dreaming bird': based on an article in *Science* magazine, November 2000.

'William Donnegan': William Faulkner, *Light in August*. William Donnegan, a member of the Niagara Movement, was murdered in 1908.

'Babak': based on a protest against the forced detention

imposed on asylum seekers by the Australian government under John Howard. Babak is a fictional character placed in an all too real situation. The nursing sister who stood against the system (at another such camp) was, I am proud to say, my wife Bet. The plight of refugees seeking asylum in Australia remains an unresolved national disgrace.

'The flame priest': the anonymous Anglo-Saxon poet of *The Wanderer*.

'Winter campaign': Hermann Broch, *The Death of Virgil*. Drawing on material from both Frederick the Great (*Military Instruction*, translated into English in 1797) and Napoleon (*Military Maxims*, published in 1827).

'The experiment': Samuel Beckett, *Mercier and Camier*.

'A couple': Joseph Furphy, *Such Is Life*.

'Sunken liner': Gabriel García Márquez, *The Autumn of the Patriarch*.

'The Beefsteak Room': Henry James, *The Wings of the Dove*. This meeting did indeed take place on 9 July 1886, as recorded by Bram Stoker himself, when Sir Richard

Burton was induced to recount the famous anecdote again.

'Querencía': an incident witnessed personally (and filmed by Ian Dixon) in 2000. *Querencía* is a word I first encountered in a poem by Thomas W. Shapcott.

'Modesty': Gertrude Stein, *Blood on the Dining-Room Floor*. The letter material is based on Darwin's account of his travels in Chile in 1834 in *A Journal of Researches*. Emma's interior monologue is entirely imagined. They married in 1839.

'Knots, ties, etc.': quoted from Commander J. Irving's revision of J. Tom Burgess's *Knots, Ties and Splices* of 1884.

'Noise': Charles Dickens, *Bleak House*. At Myall Creek the massacre of defenceless Aboriginal people in 1838 was committed by eleven convicts—some still serving their sentences as unpaid rural labourers, others as ticket-of-leavers having partial freedom—who were eventually brought to trial in New South Wales by Governor Sir George Gipps. A twelfth murderer, their leader, John Fleming, the only freeborn man among them, was never caught nor brought to trial. Such was the class system. He himself and his atrocious crime were real enough, but his fear of silence and his shield of noise are my invention—in fact nothing seems to be known of him apart from his name.

'Li River': Malcolm Lowry, *Under the Volcano*. The reference is to the film of Somerset Maugham's novel, *The Painted Veil*.

'Book burial': Wolfgang Borchert, *The Man Outside*. Based on a factual event still shrouded in secrecy. One evening the East German parliament accepted that the cost of patrolling the Berlin Wall was no longer sustainable—that it could no longer afford itself—and the troops were withdrawn. This was the signal. Almost immediately people began to scale the abandoned wall and to break it down, while on both sides the partying began. The attempted burial of communist ideology followed. Concerning the tradition of burning books and the length of time this requires, it is said that when Caliph Umar destroyed the ancient library at Alexandria (already decimated by Christians) the scrolls took six months to burn. The mention of Time Forms refers to Giambattista Vico's *The New Science* of 1744.

'AD 1000': King Alfred the Great, *Orosius*. Developed from an idea suggested by a woodcut in an original book from the Gutenberg Press at the National Gallery of Victoria.

'Winners': Louis-Ferdinand Céline, *Death on the Installment Plan*. A street scene witnessed in Chapel Street, Prahran, Melbourne on 17 December 2010.

'Glider pilot': A tribute to my uncle, Ralph Buckland.

'TV reporter', the transcription of a dream, was first published in my collection of prose fragments, *The Most Beautiful World* (UQP, 1981), 'Street scene', 'Babak' and 'John Fleming' were first published in earlier versions in *Griffith Review 26* and 'Semaphore' was published in the *Good Weekend* magazine of the *Sydney Morning Herald* and the Melbourne *Age*.

Acknowledgements

I am grateful for help offered me during the years when these fictions were written. Thanks to Julian Burnside and Kate Durham for repeated kindnesses, Neilma Gantner, Barbara Blackman, The Bundanon Trust and Victoria University—to Bet for so many shaping memories and to our darling daughters Imogen, Delia and Cressida—and to Dylan Warren for his exacting responses to the work in progress.

Thanks also to my agent, Mary Cunnane, to my publisher at Pier 9, Melanie Ostell, and to my editor, Ali Lavau.

Also available by the author, *popeye never told you*

'Do not be misled by the "Childhood Memories" of the
subtitle. Self-indulgent nostalgia is nowhere to be found in this
book, which is a richly novelistic saga of a wartime family in
Britain. It is Rodney Hall's genius that his story evokes strong
personal memories in the mind of the reader ... To read this
book is a double pleasure: we enter both the world of young
Rod and our own childhood at the same time ... I didn't want
this book to end.'
Craig Munro, *Australian Book Review*

'Rodney Hall is a magnificently perceptive and venturesome
writer ... his memoir is written in the simple words and halting
prose of a child. Through this experiment Hall explores the
possibility of finding the past, and capturing the voice and
perspective of a young child.'
Canberra Times

'An accessible and beautifully written memoir.'
Good Reading

Hardback ISBN 9781741967593 rrp$29.99
ebook ISBN 9781742667607 rrp$24.99

RODNEY HALL

popeye never told you

childhood memories of the war

'Everything about
Rodney Hall's work is
major: the beauty of the
writing, the dark and
vibrant imagination,
and the enormous
pleasure it gives the
reader' MICHAEL HERR

'A thrillingly smart
and juicy writer'
NEW YORK TIMES